Romance On A Deserted Island – Or Is It?

Written by Janet Kay Blaylock

Edited by Brenda Willmore

Copyright Page

This book is fictional, so any names, places, or incidents are a product of the author's creative imagination. Any resemblance to anyone living or dead is a coincidence.

No part of this book shall be used in any form or copied without written permission to the author and publisher, Janet Blaylock.

Preface

Penny Marshall lived in California and because of some recent trials in her life, she wanted to escape to some place far away, so she chose Lakeview (a fictitious city). It took her three days to travel in her van and her travel trailer, which had all of the conveniences of a mobile home.

When she arrived in Lakeview, she found a campsite and a spot in a secluded area where she could camp until she found an apartment. She left her trailer in the campsite and took her van.

The suspense starts to build when Penny came home and found a body in her bathtub. Penny stared at the body and dashed out of the apartment and down to Abby's apartment. That night, Penny gathered a few of her things and spent the night with Abby. Early the next morning, Penny went to her apartment and found a threatening note. She gathered a few more things and then returned to Abby's apartment, packed up her belongings, and left without saying anything to Abby.

When Detective Mallory came over to speak to Penny, Abby found out she had disappeared. They didn't know what to think.

Cedar Tree Mysteries

Cedar Tree Mysteries features Christy and Megan Parker, who are twins. Their adventures begin when they enter the second grade and will continue throughout their lives as adults. The series will also feature other characters who will join them in their book club titled *Cedar Tree Mysteries Book Club*.

There are three levels in *Cedar Tree Mysteries*: Elementary Readers, Middle Readers, Young Adult Readers to Adult Readers. The following list is what is included in the series at this time as well as other books by Janet Kay Blaylock:

Elementary Readers - Ages 7 to 9

Cedar Tree Mysteries Book Club

Solving Mysteries

Middle Readers - Ages 10 to 12

Strange Happenings

Young Adult to Adult Readers - Ages 13 and up

Romance On A Deserted Island – Or Is It

Secret of Cedar Tree Mansion

The Kidnapping

Chapter One
A New Experience

"I've had it with these circumstances!" Penny Marshall blurted out, as she threw her glass of water across the room and watched it shatter into small pieces on the kitchen floor. "If only he had just left me alone instead of interrogating me, I would have been satisfied, but now I have to abandon my life and my home where I've been happy and content and take up residence in another city far away from here."

Penny couldn't comprehend what led up to the unhappiness she experienced the past few months because she thought things were all right until now. As a result, she became upset and realized there wasn't a way out because she thought her life wasn't going to improve, so she decided to move even though she enjoyed living in her new home and in California.

"Where do I go since I have to abandon my home in California and relocate somewhere else?" Penny asked herself.

She walked into the living room and picked up her pamphlets on various places that sounded interesting. She originally wanted the pamphlets so she could become acquainted with various cities because she wanted to use them in the settings for her short stories. Now, she had to relocate so she was glad that she had the pamphlets. She wanted to select the right location for her to live at least temporarily. Penny browsed through the brochures and spotted a place named Lakeview (a fictitious city) that looked intriguing and read the information about the city. As she read the pamphlet, she decided that it sounded like a fantastic place to live, so she took her red marker and circled Lakeview on the front of the pamphlet, and then she tossed them on her desk.

She glanced at the clock on her desk and realized that she needed to start packing because she wanted to leave before her neighbors got off work, and it started getting dark. She didn't want any of her neighbors to see her leaving.

Even though Penny couldn't comprehend why things happened the way they did, she believed there was a reason for what happened, and she anticipated her new experiences that she might encounter in Lakeview. She was optimistic about her life and believed she would eventually realize what had gone awry in her life, but as she thought about moving to an unknown place, anxieties started to overwhelm her.

Tears flowed down her cheeks, as she blurted out. "Why did this happen? Who am I? Why can't people leave me alone and accept me as Penny Marshal. That's who I am. My past doesn't matter anymore."

Penny grabbed the sofa pillows and threw them across the living room. Then, she tossed off the papers and things on top of her desk. She didn't care how the room looked because she was going to leave and not return. She wanted to take her clothes, her computers, her writing supplies, and books.

When Penny calmed down, she noticed the pamphlets and picked them up. Then, she plopped onto the blue plush sofa so she could browse through them again just to make sure that Lakeview was the right location for her. As she read through the pamphlet about Lakeview, she discovered that there were three separate campsites with large lakes, so this confirmed to her that she made the right decision, since she enjoyed camping and being near the water. She also couldn't imagine how anyone would discover where she planned to relocate since it was a long way from California.

Penny returned the pamphlets to the desk and then walked into her bedroom so she could start packing her suitcases in order to leave before her neighbors returned home from work.

As Penny stood inside her bedroom and glanced around the room, tears flowed down her cheeks. "Why? Why did this happen to me? I don't want to move! It's not right," Penny blurted out, as she grabbed a tissue and wiped the tears that flooded her eyes and rolled down her cheeks.

Penny was too devastated about her circumstances because this was the last time she was going to occupy her newly decorated house. The bedroom, which was the master bedroom, had her favorite colors, light blue, navy blue, and yellow. She had a double bed with a bookcase headboard where she kept her most favorite books, and her bed had a navy blue bedspread with yellow daisies.

She also had two chests, a dresser with six drawers below and a rectangular mirror above, two lamp tables that had gold lamps with white shades, a walk-in closet, large desk with drawers, and two light blue cushioned armchairs. Her windows had pale yellow blinds and navy blue silk curtains along the side and across the top. The walls were light blue, and a navy blue shag carpet covered the floor.

She also had a full bathroom with an Oakwood vanity that had two doors below the two marble top lavatories above, a drawer below, and inside the vanity were two small drawers and a space for bath tissue or cleaning supplies.

Penny grabbed an empty box and placed her books that were in her bookcase headboard inside the box. With tears in her eyes and anger building up inside, she tossed the pillows on her bed and her bedspread on the floor. "Why?" Penny blurted out and cried. "It's not fair. Why me?"

After Penny opened the door to her spacious walk-in closet, she grabbed her two large turquoise suitcases that she kept on the carpet and placed them on the bed so she could pack her clothes. When Penny walked back to the closet, she had to search for her matching medium suitcase and her cosmetic case because she thought she had kept them beside the two larger ones. She had to move several items in order to look in the back of the closet. Finally, she located the medium suitcase on the floor and the cosmetic case on the top shelf toward the back of the closet.

Penny placed her suitcases on her bed and opened one of the large suitcases so she could put her slacks inside, she walked back to the closet and grabbed a handful of slacks and shorts. She laid them on the bed, took her clothes off the yellow plastic hangers and carefully folded her clothes so they wouldn't wrinkle too much.

Since the trip would take three days to arrive in Lakeview, she decided to keep what she needed for those days in her smaller suitcase that she still had in the closet, so it would be handy. She walked back to the closet to search for it and found it in the back where the medium suitcase had been, so she picked it up off the floor and laid it on the bed in order to place a few slacks outfits in it.

Since it was spring and the wind blew throughout the day, which made it cooler outside, she decided to wear slacks, so after she opened her suitcase, she searched through her slacks to see what would be appropriate to wear in the cooler weather. Finally, she selected her purple slacks, a matching jacket, and a lavender shirt; her rust colored slacks, a matching vest, and a pale yellow shirt; and her brown slacks, a matching sweater, and a cream-colored shirt, and then she carefully folded each outfit and placed them inside the smaller suitcase.

After that, she packed her personal items she would need for those three days on the road and placed them inside the smaller suitcase. Because Penny enjoyed being outside and camping, she planned on parking at a campsite each of those days so she could stay inside her conventional travel trailer when she became too exhausted to continue driving instead of searching for a motel.

Since her conventional travel trailer had all the conveniences she needed to live such as a kitchen area, living area, appliances, toilet facilities, and a sleeping area; she wanted to stay in there instead of a motel.

When she finished packing her slacks and shorts, she returned to her closet to get her blouses and skirts and as soon as she had one suitcase packed, she opened up her other large navy blue suitcase and packed more clothes in that one.

Then, she opened up her medium suitcase and placed her nightwear and other personal items that were in her chest of drawers in the suitcase. After she had her clothes packed, she opened the dresser drawers, took out her cosmetics and other items, and placed them in her cosmetic suitcase.

As soon as, she packed her small cosmetic suitcase, she opened her closet door, chest of drawers, and dresser to make sure she had removed everything, and then she walked into the garage to get a large box with a lid. After she entered her bedroom, she placed all of her shoes and slippers inside the box and placed the lid on top.

Since she wasn't going to return to California, she wanted to gather all of her belongings now. When she had everything packed, she picked up her two large suitcases, walked outside to her van, and put them in the back. Then, she walked back inside to load the other ones, and when she had her suitcases in the van, she rushed into the house to pack up her laptop, her desktop computer, and her supplies.

As she unhooked her computer, printer, monitor, keyboard, speakers, and mouse, tears came to her eyes again. She pondered over the different possibilities as to why this happened in her life when she thought everything was perfect. She hoped that someday she would be happy again. After she put her desktop computer and supplies in a large box, she placed her laptop inside its case and packed up her computer accessories in another small bag. She carried her suitcases to the car and walked back inside to get her laptop and bag of computer accessories. Penny knew she wouldn't return, so she cleaned out the items in her desk drawers and put them in a box.

She packed them into boxes and carried them to her van. In addition to her clothes and computers, she decided to take a small bookcase, a small writing table, a comfortable desk chair, and two lamps to her van. She hated to leave the rest of the furniture, but she didn't have enough room in her van and trailer for everything, so she took the most important things and would purchase the other things.

Penny knew she had plenty of time to pack her van and trailer, but she still didn't want to be too leisurely in her packing just in case something happened unexpectedly. She also knew she had to leave without anyone seeing her because she didn't want any of her neighbors to know that she was leaving or which direction she was headed in case someone followed her.

As she walked into her kitchen, she remembered that she needed to take her cooler and food since she hadn't planned on stopping anywhere on the way, except for rest stops, so she walked downstairs to get her cooler. Then, she walked back upstairs to search through the food in the pantry to see what she had wanted to take with her, but she knew that she needed to leave some things.

She filled her cooler with ice packs to keep her food cold, and then she added her cheese sticks, yogurts, containers of cream cheese, fudge, brownies, and the ham salad sandwiches that she made earlier that day for her trip.

After that, she took out a couple of paper sacks and filled them up with her potato chips, crackers, chocolate chip cookies, chocolate cupcakes, and pretzel sticks. She took her cooler and her two paper sacks of snacks to the trailer and put some of the perishables inside her refrigerator. Before she left for Lakeview, she walked back inside the house to make sure she had everything she wanted to take.

Penny was still upset, so she continued to throw a few things on the floor just to make it look like an intruder entered her house. Maybe someone would wonder what happened to the place and to her. Then, she shut her front door and locked it.

Since Penny was a freelance writer, she worked at home and most of her neighbors were gone during the day, so she could leave anytime she wanted.

As she climbed into her van, she glanced around the neighborhood to see if anyone happened to be nearby or in case someone got off work earlier than she expected. She was relieved when she didn't notice anyone, so she cautiously backed out of the driveway. Even though it was difficult for Penny to leave her house, she knew that she had to abandon her life in California and take up a new residence in Lakeview.

Penny thought about her life as she headed toward Texas. *I'm relieved that I decided to move to Lakeview, and that I changed my name to Penny Marshall even though I don't know why I chose that name. At least I changed it before my first book came out last month so people wouldn't recognize me.*

After driving for several hours and through the desert, Penny became exhausted and needed to stop for the night. She drove around until she spotted a rest area, so she drove into the entrance and noticed a secluded area nearby. She parked her van and climbed out so she could stretch her legs. "The cool breeze is so relaxing,"

Penny said to herself, as the cool evening breeze brushed across her face. She looked up at the sky and saw that it was clear. "I'm glad I could walk around for a few minutes because I get tired driving a long way without breaks."

Penny walked into her trailer and opened a window slightly so the night air could filter through her trailer while she slept. Then, she locked her trailer door, opened her refrigerator and took out a ham salad sandwich and a can of pop.

While she sat on her bed and ate, she picked up her favorite anthology mystery book that had themes of impossible mysteries and read for a half hour before she put on her flannel blue flowered night-shirt.

As she lay in bed, she thought about her mystery book and wished she could meet a girl in her new environment who wanted to start a mystery book club with her. She thought it would be exciting to read mysteries with another girl friend and to solve some mysteries in real life like the detectives she read about in her books.

Early the next morning, Penny woke up, put on her brown slacks, cream-colored shirt, her brown sweater, her socks and athletic shoes, grabbed a cinnamon roll, and some orange juice, and then walked outside and locked her trailer, so she could stroll around the area. "I like the fresh scents of the flowers when they start to bloom in the springtime, and I like to watch the cedar trees, oak trees, and cherry trees when they start to blossom. The birds seem happy as they sing their melodies in the trees."

Penny heard some American Robins singing different melodies in the black cherry trees, and a few minutes later, she saw sparrows and wrens flying among the trees. A half hour later, she strolled back to her van and unlocked it so she could continue her trip.

As Penny continued to travel, she wanted her window down because there was a slight breeze, and she wanted to continue to smell the fresh flowers and to listen to the American Robins singing their melodies. "I can't believe I'm traveling all this way by myself.

This is my first time to travel alone, and it feels good, but at the same time it feels scary because of the things that could happen to someone who is traveling alone." Tears started to roll down Penny's cheeks as she thought about being alone and traveling to a place where she hadn't been. "I miss my home in California. I wonder what is happening now, and if someone noticed that I disappeared. With the way I left the house, I wonder if people would think an intruder entered and took me away. Who knows what will happen."

After traveling several hours, she located another rest spot and pulled into the entrance so she could park her van in a secluded spot surrounded by oak trees. She preferred parking in areas where nobody would notice her because she didn't want anyone to recognize her, especially someone from California, but even though she was positive nobody saw her leave, she still wanted to be cautious. She climbed out of her van, locked it, and then walked into her trailer and locked that door. After she opened her refrigerator to get another sandwich and pop, she opened her bag where she had her snacks and took out a can of potato chips. She sat in her kitchen area, so she could eat her supper and read in her mystery book again until it was time to get ready for bed.

The early morning sunlight that shone through Penny's window startled her, so she climbed out of bed and donned her rust colored slacks, matching vest, and cream-colored shirt. After that, she walked over to her refrigerator to get out her strawberry yogurt, and then she opened a drawer in the kitchen area, took out a spoon, and sat at the table to eat. When she finished eating, she disposed her trash and opened the door to her trailer, so she could walk outside to stretch her legs and to stroll around for a few minutes before she climbed into her van to finish her trip to Lakeview.

She looked forward to her new environment and wondered what it would be like or about her new apartment. She wanted to get one by Monday.

Penny arrived in Lakeview an hour later, and the first thing she wanted to do was to search for a campsite because she was eager to rest before she began searching for a place to live. Within a few minutes, Penny found a campsite just west of the city limits of Lakeview.

As she drove through the main entrance, she noticed a secluded area not too far from the entrance, so she parked her van and opened her door to stretch her legs. She still wanted to be safe and secure even though she was several miles from California. "I'm glad I finally arrived in Lakeview. I just hope this is a better place."

As she walked around her new environment, she listened to the American Robins singing in the trees and smelled the fresh spring flowers, and then noticed a lake with an island in the middle. When Penny returned to her trailer, she unlocked her door because she wanted her privacy, and she wanted to think about her plans. "This is going to be difficult at first because of the new experience of living alone, but at least I didn't have a full-time occupation I had to resign in order to move to Lakeview. Since I'm a freelance writer, I am a freelance writer, I can continue with my writing no matter where I live."

Penny opened up her laptop case and took out her laptop so she could start writing to her e-mail friend, Crimesolver, which was a username. Penny thought Crimesolver was an interesting name for someone who was an amateur detective. Penny's username was Crimewriter because she wrote crime fiction stories and books as well as the subgenres such as mysteries, suspense, and detective fiction.

Since Penny didn't know Crimesolver's real name or her location, she felt safer to meet someone over the Internet even though that caused her recent problems. Penny wasn't sure she wanted to make new friends in person after what happened to her in California or at least right away, but she liked writing to Crimesolver by e-mail, and she thought about asking her if she wanted to get together for an e-mail mystery book club. Then, later on, they could meet in person as she began to trust people.

Penny liked her idea about reading mysteries together, discussing the detectives, and solving mysteries in real life like the detectives in the mysteries she read.

Crimewriter's E-mail Letter

"Hi, Crimesolver, how are you? I've had a difficult few weeks lately and have been depressed, but I made a major decision in my life, so I hope things will improve soon. I'm staying at a campsite in a secluded spot for a few days because it's quiet and peaceful here. I don't see any other campers nearby, so I can work on my freelance writing without being interrupted, and I can smell the fresh spring flowers and trees as well as listen to the robins singing in the black cherry trees. Spring is my favorite season because the flowers are blooming, as well as the leaves appearing on the trees.

I just had my first mystery book published, so I'm living off my royalties and the money I had been saving for my move. Have you solved any special cases lately?

By the way, I've thought about starting a mystery book club because I thought it would be exciting to read mysteries together and to see how the detectives solve crimes. I've been interested in becoming an amateur detective like you someday after I locate a place to live and have organized it.

This will be a difficult adjustment for me since I'll be living on my own now, but I'm confident I can handle my new situation."

Penny sent her e-mail and hoped that Crimesolver would respond before too long. They tried to set up a regular time where they could write to each other, but since Penny made her decision to move, she didn't have time to write to her for the last few days. However, she knew Crimesolver understood that she planned to move out of state, but she didn't reveal where she wanted to relocate.

Within a half hour, Penny received an e-mail letter from Crimesolver, so she opened it and read it. "That was fast. I sure like hearing from Crimesolver. I hope we can meet someday, but for right now I don't want to meet anyone in person, and I don't know how that would happen since we haven't revealed our identity or location."

Crimesolver's E-mail Letter

"Hi, Crimewriter, I have a new case about a child who has been missing since she was two years old, which was twenty years ago, and there hasn't been any information about her since that time. It seems like she just vanished off the face of the earth. I don't know what happened to her, but the police want me to see if I can find out anything on my computer. Her real parents have continued to search for her."

Crimewriter's E-mail Letter

"Hi, Crimesolver. That sounds like a difficult case, but I'm positive you'll find the missing girl so you can bring her family together soon. It must be difficult on her parents to have her missing for such a long time, too.

I'll write again tomorrow because I want to get my life together and to explore my new environment. I'd like to locate a place near a bookstore, so I can shop on a regular basis and not have too far to go.

I want to purchase some mystery anthologies, so I can become acquainted with various authors."

Penny turned off her laptop and opened her refrigerator to get out a ham sandwich and a can of pop for supper. As she ate, she thought about Crimesolver and the case she was working on. "I wonder who disappeared and why? That's such a long time to be away from your parents. They must be devastated," Penny said, to herself. After she ate, she wrote in her journal.

Crimewriter's Journal

Several children have disappeared at an early age, so I feel sorry for the parents because they don't know what happened to their children. I don't understand why parents don't keep a closer watch on their children so they don't disappear, but on the other hand, some parents are too strict with their children because they don't want them to do anything except stay at home. It makes me wonder why they wanted to have children in the beginning if they have trouble keeping track of their children or are too strict. Parents should allow children to get out and develop friendships with their school peers, so I don't understand why my parents wanted to teach me at home instead of letting me go to school. As a result, I didn't have any friends.

"I wonder where Crimesolver lives because it would be good to meet her someday, but on the other hand, I'm not sure I'm ready to meet anyone. I've been hurt too much," Penny said to herself, as she cried. "Why is this happening to me? I miss California, but I can't forget what happened to me."

Penny reached for a tissue and wiped the tears from her eyes. Then she ate supper. After that, she turned off her light and went to bed because she was extremely tired after her trip from California, and she wanted to arise early to walk around the campsite.

Penny also wanted to drive around Lakeview to observe her new surroundings, and to find an apartment she liked so she could start her new life and forget about her past. Even though she moved far away, she thought she would be safe and wouldn't run into anyone from California.

Penny arose early Monday morning and donned her navy blue slacks, light blue blouse, a navy blue vest, and her white socks and athletic shoes.

As she looked through her snacks, she realized that she needed to purchase some groceries today because she didn't have many things left. In addition to her cooler, Penny had the regular appliances such as a stove, refrigerator, and microwave so she could cook and eat in her travel trailer. She was happy that she had those appliances because she had more room to keep her perishable items like ham and cheese sandwiches, yogurts, cheese sticks, several cans of pop, and some bottles of spring water in the refrigerator than she did in the cooler. Penny liked fixing food that was convenient because she wanted to spend more time writing than she did cooking and doing dishes. She wanted to get another book written and published soon.

After Penny finished her strawberry yogurt and orange juice, she walked outside to stretch her legs, get some fresh air, and to look around the campsite. She noticed a lake and an island in the middle of the lake, so she thought this campsite would be a great place for her to stay because she might like to travel out to the island and stay there sometime. She thought it would be a safe place to stay for a few days because nobody could locate her. There weren't any other campers nearby, so she felt relieved about that because she could have some solitary time.

However, she realized she would need to purchase a boat in order to travel to the island, so she decided to shop for a one as soon as she had a place to live. Penny anticipated her new experience in Lakeview. "I still need to find an apartment," Penny said to herself. "Since this is a secluded area, I can leave my travel trailer here and just drive my van." She unhooked her trailer, climbed inside her van, headed out of the campsite toward the city limits of Lakeview.

As she drove toward the city limits, she glanced from side to side looking at the scenery and the different buildings. She wanted to become familiar with the area, so she could remember where her campsite was located. A short distance from the campsite where she stayed, she spotted a shopping center and a couple of apartment complexes that were located on the opposite side of the shopping center. Stopping to search for a place to turn into the shopping center, she felt something hit her from behind. When she glanced through her rear view mirror, she realized that the car behind her hit her van. Feeling angry inside, she turned off her engine and jumped out of her van. "Thanks for hitting my van!" Penny blurted out, as she brushed a strand of her shoulder length brown hair, which used to be longer and blonde, away from her face.

"I'm sorry for bumping into your van, but I didn't expect you to stop in the middle of the street," the woman replied. She was a slender young looking woman and looked attractive in her brown slacks, beige blouse, and brown vest.

"Maybe you need to pay more attention!" Penny snapped, as she brushed another strand of her brown hair away from her face. Penny's heart raced and anxiety overwhelmed her because she was afraid of what might happen next since she knew she caused the accident.

Even though Penny realized she caused the incident by stopping in the middle of the street, she wanted to blame the other driver, and she wanted to admit that she hadn't been to Lakeview before today, so she wasn't familiar with the area. She hoped she wouldn't get in trouble. In addition to being afraid of what might happen, she was also afraid of meeting anyone, and she didn't want to confront anyone from California.

Shortly, the police arrived. "What happened here?" Detective Rowland asked, as he approached the two women. Detective Rowland, who was about 5'7"and average weight, had on his light blue uniform and cap as well as his pistol.

"I accidentally hit her van from behind because she suddenly stopped in the middle of the street, and I didn't expect her to stop where she did. I tried to stop, but I couldn't and ended up hitting her car," the other driver responded. "I'm sorry it happened, and I'll be glad to pay for any repairs she has as a result of the accident."

"I haven't been to Lakeview before and couldn't see where to turn into this shopping center. That's why I stopped in the middle of the street like I did," Penny replied, as she relaxed a little bit.

"I need to see both of your driver's licenses," Detective Rowland said.

"My name's Penny," she said, as she handed Detective Rowland her driver's license.

"My name's Abby," she said, as she handed Detective Rowland her information. "Like I mentioned earlier, I'll be happy to pay for her repairs."

"I can pay for my own," Penny replied.

"It's just a fender bender, so it's not going to cost much to fix your cars," Detective Rowland said. "However, I will have to give you a warning for inattentive drive, Miss Fisher, as he looked at her driver's license." Detective Rowland took out his pen and pad to write down the information.

"Miss Marshall, you can get your van fixed in this shopping center. Just turn in here," Detective Rowland said, as he pointed to the entrance of the shopping mall.

"Thanks," Penny said, a little calmer.

"If you want to pay for her car repairs, Miss Fisher, that's fine," Detective Rowland replied.

"Since she's going in here, I can get my car fixed here, too," Miss Fisher replied.

"This time, I'm letting you off with a warning, Miss Fisher, but next time please be more careful. Also, Miss Marshall, I know you're new to Lakeview, but it's better to drive slowly and cautiously since you aren't sure of your surroundings."

"I will," Penny replied.

Penny climbed into her van and drove to the service station so she could get some gas and then get her van repaired. A young looking man dressed in blue jeans and a white short sleeve shirt came to wait on Penny. Penny told him she had a fender bender a few minutes ago.

"I'll be happy to help you, Miss Marshall."

"What? Who said my name was Miss Marshall?"

"It was the other woman, Miss Fisher. She told me she bumped into your van and wanted to pay for your gas and to fix your van."

"Why? I can afford it," Penny snapped.

"She wanted to do it for you," the service attendant said. "By the way, I'm Ben Walker."

"Okay."

"You look familiar. How long have you lived here?"

"I came here last night, but right now I'm in a hurry, so can you fix my van soon?"

"It will take me an hour to fix your fender, so you can wait here if you want to."

"I'll just look around the shopping center, so I'll be back in an hour."

"Okay," Ben said, as he filled up Penny's van with gas. After that, he took her van into the garage to repair it.

Without saying another word to him or to Abby, Penny looked at the names of the different stores as she started walking around the shopping center. Within a few minutes, she spotted a bookstore.

Penny enjoyed browsing around bookstores because she liked reading mysteries and writing short stories, books, and book reviews, and she came up with some ideas for her stories by reading mysteries.

Penny walked down the mystery section and browsed through the books until she located a mystery that just came out. To her surprise, she saw her mystery book among the collection of new books on display, so she picked up her book and looked at it. The back inside cover had her picture and a short biography, and the front inside cover had a summary of her book.

Her first book came out last month, which was March, so she was excited about having her first book published. She walked to the checkout stand to pay for her book.

"You look familiar. Have you lived in Lakeview long?" the cashier asked.

"No. I came here last night," Penny replied.

"Oh. I'm Annie Walker."

"Okay. Bye."

Penny walked outside and toward the grocery store and wondered who those people were and why they kept saying she looked familiar to them when she didn't know them.

After that, she walked to the grocery store and picked up some more snacks: cheese sticks, yogurts, club crackers, ham, cream cheese, bread, and two cartons of pop. Then, she walked up to the counter.

"Good morning. How are you?" the cashier asked.

"Okay."

"That's good. By the way, you look familiar. How long have you lived here?"

"I came here last night," Penny replied.

"You look familiar, but I'm not sure where I've seen you," the cashier commented.

Penny gathered up her two sacks and walked out the door. She still couldn't believe how these people kept saying she looked familiar to them when she just arrived in Lakeview. This situation seemed mysterious to her, and she knew she had to do something because she didn't want anyone recognizing her. Her purpose for moving was to escape from the people she knew in California, and now people seem to know her here. "What is it with these people who claim I look familiar to them? What's going on? I just changed my appearance, but maybe I need to change something again."

She walked back to her van and found out that it was ready, so she put her groceries and book inside and drove to the salon because she had to do something with her hair to make herself different so people wouldn't recognize her.

When she entered the beauty salon, she saw a young looking woman. "Good morning. May I help you?" the woman asked.

"I want to do something different with my hair, but I'm not sure what."

"Do you want a different hair style or color?" the woman asked.

"I just want to change my appearance somehow."

"Have you thought about a wig?" the hair stylist asked.

"No, but that might solve my problem. Where can I purchase a wig?"

"We have some wigs here for sale. They're in the back, so if you wait here, I'll bring some out to show you." The hair stylist went to the back room and returned with a few wigs of different styles and colors.

"These are great!" Penny exclaimed. I like them, but I think these two will work for me because I can have different styles and colors when I need to change my appearance."

"These two, the blonde wig and the brown wig," the hair stylist responded, as she gave Penny the wigs.

"Yes. They will be great for me," Penny replied. *I hope that, people won't recognize me,* Penny thought.

"Okay. These two will look good on you, and they are different styles as well as colors. I hope you will be satisfied with these wigs."

"I like my own hair and style, but these will work for me," Penny said.

Penny paid for the wigs, walked out the door, climbed into her van, and began her search for an apartment. She saw an apartment complex nearby, so she entered the parking lot and parked in front of the building. She climbed out of her van and walked around for a few minutes, so she could get a feel of what it might be like living there.

She didn't think it looked too bad, and it was close to the shopping center, so she decided to check it out. She entered the office and a middle-aged slender looking woman wearing green slacks, a white long sleeved blouse, and a matching green vest greeted her. "May I help you?"

"I just arrived in Lakeview last night, and I'm looking for an apartment because I'm planning on staying here," Penny replied.

"It's nice to have you here. Where did you come from?"

"California. Do you have any apartments available?" Penny asked, as she tried to change the subject because she didn't want to acknowledge any more information about her past life in California.

That was her personal life, and she wanted to forget it.

"I just have one apartment available, so I'd be happy to show it to you if you'd like," the woman answered, as she smiled. "By the way, what brought you all the way from California to Lakeview?"

"That would be great," Penny replied, politely, as she ignored the other question. "I'd like to see the apartment." However, Penny wasn't sure she'd like renting an apartment in this complex because of the way the outside looked as well as the inside.

It was apparent to her that someone had neglected the place because the windows needed replacing and the trim needed painting. In addition to the repairs and painting on the outside, Penny noticed that someone needed to do some repairing and painting on the inside so the place would look more attractive to people.

The walls had a drab color and looked like they hadn't had a coat of fresh paint for several years, and she thought the office needed some fresh plants, different types of magazines, a pop machine, snack machine, and comfortable chairs for people. Penny wished that she could help this woman, but her responsibility was to search for an apartment.

Because of all the problems Penny noticed, she couldn't understand why someone who owned a business like this didn't do the repairs and painting that the place needed so it would look more attractive to people.

In addition to the way the apartment looked inside and outside, she couldn't see why anyone would want to rent an apartment here unless it was quite cheap.

The woman turned and grabbed the key off the rack, which was located on the wall behind the counter, and escorted Penny to the elevator up to the second floor where the room was located.

When Penny entered the room, she noticed the drab colors and the worn out, stained carpet, so she knew she didn't want to live in a place like this, but she wanted to be polite to the woman. "Thank you for showing me the apartment. Since I'm just starting to look for a place, I'd like to see what other apartments are available before I make my final decision," Penny replied.

"I understand, but I hope you don't hesitate too long because my apartments go quickly, and as I mentioned earlier, I just have one left," the woman replied, with a smile.

"That's fine. I realize that it could be rented out before I return and that's fine, but I'm one who wants to check out different possibilities before I make an important decision such as renting an apartment, so if I'm interested in it, I'll return later today."

"It's important to be sure that you have the right apartment because you wouldn't want to sign a contract for an apartment and find out you weren't happy. Thank you for stopping by," the woman replied, as she opened the front door for Penny.

"You're welcome, and thanks again for showing me the apartment," Penny said, as she walked outside to her van.

Penny climbed into her van and decided to head west toward the campsite where she stayed last night. On the way toward the campsite, she noticed a large professional looking sign printed in a bright color that read:

Lakeview Apartments. One mile south and east.

One, two, and three bedroom apartments.

Enclosed playground area for children.

Crystal Lake and picnic area across the street.

As Penny headed toward the apartment complex, she spotted it on the east side of the street. When she saw the apartment complex, she knew she had to check it out because it looked more attractive than the one she just saw, so she parked in the parking lot, and as she climbed out of the van, a gentle breeze brushed across her face.

She stood in front of the apartment complex and observed the surroundings, and then she noticed the name, Lakeview Apartments, on the first building, which was also labeled A.

Lakeview Apartments consisted of four separate buildings and were named A, B C, and D. Each building, which was white with a blue roof, had two floors, and the cedar trees that surrounded the buildings gave the tenants a feeling of security.

In the middle of the complex was a fenced-in playground area, which consisted of swings, sand pile, teeter-totter, and plastic climbing equipment, for the children who lived in the apartments. The tenants could park in carports located near their apartment building or they could park in the

spaces in front of the buildings, and the visitors and handicap people had special parking spaces in front of each building.

Penny felt comfortable with the surroundings because of the appearance of the complex, the convenience to the shopping center, and the convenience to the campsite where she stayed last night, so she had to check out this apartment complex. Since the shopping area and the apartment complex were located near the campsite, she could go camping whenever she wanted to get away.

Chapter Two
Penny's New Apartment

As Penny opened the front door, she heard the sound of a bell, which she realized was to notify the office workers and the manager that someone entered the office. Glancing around the spacious office, Penny noticed a living area to the left of the door that gave the office a peaceful and cozy feeling. The cream-colored walls brightened up the area, and the windows with the white blinds and light brown silk curtains enhanced the color scheme. A rectangular coffee table that displayed a variety of magazines was in front of a large brown leather sofa, which had two tan colored square pillows on each end. The two large green ferns in brown decorative containers that were in the corners of the room opposite of the doorway enhanced the décor. Across from the sofa and coffee table were two cream-colored cushioned armchairs, and to the right of the chairs and sofa was a brown square table with a large television. The atmosphere of this apartment building gave Penny a feeling of peace.

She walked into the main room, and as she approached the front counter, she heard the manager's door open. As she glanced towards the manager's office, she saw a man of average height and weight dressed in brown casual clothes approach the counter.

"Welcome to Lakeview Apartments. I'm Mr. Martin, the manager of Lakeview Apartments. How may I help you?" he inquired with a pleasant expression.

"I'm checking out various apartment complexes to see where I'd like to live and wondered if you had any apartments available?"

"As a matter of fact, I do have some luxurious apartments available."

"That's great. I'd like to see an apartment," Penny replied.

"I have a few apartments available in this building and a few in Building B and C, but Building D is completely filled. Any building in particular?"

"This building is fine with me since we're here, and you mentioned that you had an apartment available, if that's all right with you."

"That's fine with me. It's on the second floor."

They took the elevator to the second floor, and when the doors opened, they walked down the hall to Apartment 201. Mr. Martin opened the door and let Penny enter first.

"By the way, it's great to have such an attractive person come to Lakeview."

"Thank you for the compliment."

"You're welcome. You mentioned that you just arrived here yesterday, so where are you from?"

"California," Penny replied.

"That's a long way from here. What brought you to Lakeview?"

As Penny entered the apartment, she stood as stiff as a statue and stared at the site of the living room because it looked more attractive than she expected.

"Wow! You're right when you said you had some luxurious apartments. This looks great, and I really like the color scheme."

"I'm glad you like it."

"I do."

"Feel free to browse around the other rooms."

Penny glanced around the living room. She couldn't believe the difference in this apartment and the other apartment she previously visited. The freshly painted light pink walls brightened the living room, and the white blinds with the burgundy curtains, which draped across the top and down the sides of the windows, enhanced the color scheme of burgundy and light pink. The light burgundy carpet added to the attractiveness of the apartment. She acknowledged to herself that this is the apartment for her because it gave her a warm, cozy feeling all over.

Penny walked into the kitchen and saw that the color scheme was just as attractive as the living room. The windows had cream-colored curtains with different shades of blue and yellow flowers. She also felt the spring breeze flow through the slightly opened windows.

Everything seemed perfect, and she hoped the bedroom would be, too. She walked into the bedroom and noticed the walk-in closet, the light blue walls, navy blue curtains, white blinds, and light blue carpet. Penny's favorite colors were burgundy, blue, and yellow, so she was ecstatic at the site of the color scheme of her new apartment.

Penny returned to the living room and told Mr. Martin that she wanted the apartment, so they left and took the elevator to the first floor to his office to fill out the paper work.

"I have my van parked outside, but my trailer is parked in a campsite, so I need to get it and unpack some of the things I brought with me. I don't have a lot of furniture, but it's a start. I'll need to get a bed, dresser, chest, and some living room furniture because I couldn't bring anything large with me."

"I understand. I do have some furniture in a storage room on the second floor that you might be able to use, so if you'd like to see what I have, we can go up there now and see if you find something you can use."

"That would be fine with me, but I can't pay much for the furniture."

"I wasn't going to charge you anything for the furniture."

"Oh," Penny replied. She was a little stunned about Mr. Martin's generosity.

They took the elevator back upstairs and walked to the storage room. After Mr. Martin unlocked the door, they walked inside. Penny was amazed at seeing a twin bed, sofa, two stuffed armchairs, a desk with drawers, two bedside tables, and a kitchen table and chairs. "I could use all of these things right now," Penny said, with a smile.

"Okay. I can get a couple of my boys to move these things into your apartment."

"That would be great. I need to go back to the campsite and get the things I have, and then I'll be back."

"Okay. I'll have the furniture moved in by the time you return," Mr. Martin said.

"Thanks for your help. I appreciate it because I'm eager to get settled in my new apartment," Penny said, with a smile.

"I hope you'll like living here."

"I'm sure I will. I'll be back as soon as I can."

"That's fine."

Penny walked over to the elevator and pushed the button to the first floor. When she reached the first floor, she walked out the front entrance and to her van. After she unlocked the door and climbed inside, she headed to the campsite.

Penny arrived, parked her van, climbed out, and unlocked her trailer. She started taking out some of the items she wanted inside her apartment and put them into her van.

Within a few minutes, Penny arrived at her new apartment complex. She was eager to move into her new apartment and see the furniture Mr. Martin had for her.

Penny parked her van in front of the building, climbed out, and unlocked the back of it so she could grab a few things to take into her new apartment. After that, she entered the building, walked to the elevator, and pushed the button to the second floor.

When the elevator stopped and the door opened, Penny stared at the man who waited to enter the elevator. He was average height and weight and dressed in a light blue shirt and denim jeans.

She started to rush pass him so she could get inside her apartment, but he stopped her and asked, "Aren't you Susan Salters?"

"No," Penny replied, as she quickly hurried to find her apartment so she could escape from the guy. She unlocked the door, walked inside, and then shut it behind her.

After taking a deep breath, she thought, *Who was that guy, and how does he know me? I thought I was going to be safe here in this apartment, but now I'm not so sure since I've come across people who claimed they know me. I even had my hair cut and dyed so nobody would recognize me. I also bought a couple of wigs so I could change my appearance.*

Penny took another deep breath and thought about her apartment. She looked around and saw the furniture that Mr. Martin had taken from the storage room and put in her apartment. She liked the way things were beginning to come together for her.

Penny heard a knock on the door and trembled with fear because she didn't want it to be the man she saw at the elevator. She hoped she wouldn't run into him again since he claimed to know her.

Penny peeked through the peephole and saw Mr. Martin, so she unlocked the door and opened it. "Hi, Mr. Martin. Thanks for the furniture. It makes my apartment look more like home now."

"You're welcome. Is there anything else I can do for you?"

"Not really. I just have to get my things out of my trailer."

"I'd be happy to help you."

"Okay. If you want to, I'd appreciate the help even though I don't have a lot of things."

They walked to the elevator, and when the doors opened, Mr. Martin pushed the button to the first floor. Then, they walked outside to Penny's van. Mr. Martin carried the heavier things while Penny carried the smaller items.

When they returned to her apartment, Penny unlocked the door, and Mr. Martin set the things down while Penny took her suitcases to her bedroom.

"By the way, is the campsite west of here, the only campsite near or in Lakeview?"

"No. There are two other campsites. One is 10 miles north of here, and the other one is 10 miles east of here. They have several trees where campers can find a place that is secluded, which most campers like because they want their privacy."

"That sounds super. I'll have to check them out and see which one I like the best."

"Okay. Please let me know if I can assist you in any way."

"I will. Thanks for your help," Penny said, with a smile.

"You're welcome."

Mr. Martin left the apartment, and Penny locked the door.

Then, she walked into her bedroom and started hanging up her clothes. After she had her clothes and personal items put away, Penny walked into her living room. As she stood in the living room and stared at her new furniture, she couldn't believe she was there in her own apartment. She felt like she made the right move because she knew she couldn't stay in California the way things developed recently in her life. She had to start a different life somewhere far away, so she was glad she decided to move to Lakeview.

Penny sat on her new sofa and thought about the man she saw in front of the elevator and wondered who he was because he looked a little familiar. "Who was that guy? Something is going on, but I don't know what? Things have to work out for me in Lakeview. I don't want to move again." Penny stood up and thought about supper because of her hunger pains, but she realized that she didn't buy too much at the grocery store since she didn't have an apartment at that time. She decided to eat what she had in her cooler that she brought with her and go to the grocery store tomorrow.

She walked into the kitchen and took out her ham and cheese sandwich, potato chips, and a pop. Then, she sat in the living room to relax. As Penny sat there and ate, she wished she had a small television set. Since she only had one television in her home in California, and it was too big, she couldn't bring it, so she needed to wait until she could purchase one.

Just as she finished eating her supper, she heard a knock on the door. When she opened it, she saw Mr. Martin with a small television set. "Hi, Miss Marshall. I have this color television set for you, too."

"Wow! Thanks. I just thought about how I'd like to have a television set." She opened the door wider so he could enter.

"I remembered you didn't have one, so I wanted you to have this one. It was in the storage." He set the television on a small table in the corner where the hook-up was located. Then, he turned it on to make sure it worked.

"I appreciate everything you've done for me," Penny said, with a smile.

"You're welcome. I enjoy helping people," Mr. Martin replied.

After Mr. Martin left, Penny locked the door and turned off her living room light. She walked into her bedroom to get ready for bed. *Even though I miss California, I'm happy with my new apartment, so I hope things work out for me here because Lakeview seems like a nice place.* Penny put on her blue flowered pajamas, walked into her bathroom to brush her teeth, and then walked back to her bed. As soon as she was in bed, she picked up her journal, which was on top of her bedside table, and wrote what happened in her life the past few days. She enjoyed keeping a journal about the events of her life because she also came up with some story ideas.

Crimewriter's Journal

Why do I look familiar to these people, and especially the guy who said I was Susan Salters. Maybe they found out I disappeared and someone notified other states.

I hope this apartment complex is safe because I don't want to confront anyone from California. I wanted to escape from people and the problems I had there. I don't want to move again because I'm happy here. I need to be careful about meeting people. On the other hand, it might be nice to meet people. That would help get my mind off the problems in California. Oh no! What if someone is using a disguise or more than one disguise? That will make things even more

36

complicated for me. I also don't want to come across the woman who bumped into my car.

After Penny finished writing in her journal, she put it on her bedside table. Then, she picked up her new mystery book and read a couple of chapters before she put it on her bedside table beside her journal. As her eyes grew drowsy, she knew it was time to turn off her light and go to sleep.

Chapter Three
The Bookstore

Early Tuesday morning, Penny woke up and turned on her lamp that was on her Oakwood bedside table. She saw her mystery book that she bought at the bookstore and decided to return to the bookstore after breakfast so she could look for other mystery books in the series and maybe another series because mysteries intrigued her.

Penny tossed off her light burgundy cozy blankets so she could climb out of her warm comfortable bed, take a shower, wash her hair, and get dressed.

After her warm shower, she donned her navy blue slacks, light blue short-sleeved blouse, matching navy blue vest, white cotton socks, athletic shoes, and one of her wigs. As soon as she was dressed, she made her bed and cleaned up her room because she always wanted her rooms to look neat and orderly in case she had visitors.

When she finished cleaning her room, she walked into the kitchen, opened the refrigerator, and decided to cook some turkey bacon, scrambled eggs, and biscuits. Penny opened up the bottom drawer in her white stove where she stored a few of her pans for baking and removed her round baking pan for her biscuits so she could cook them. After that, she opened up the can of biscuits, placed all ten biscuits a few inches apart inside the pan, and put the pan in the oven. While her biscuits cooked, she opened up her cupboard, took out the microwavable bacon plate that had ridges for the grease, placed her bacon slices on the plate, and put them in the microwave. As the biscuits and bacon were cooking, she took out the orange juice and poured some in a light blue plastic glass so she could drink a few sips while she started cooking her eggs.

When her breakfast was ready, she placed her food on a white plate with blue and yellow flowers and sat down at the square kitchen table that had a light blue tablecloth on it and a small white vase of navy blue and yellow flowers in the center. She picked up her fork with yellow plastic handles, but she remembered she wanted her window slightly opened. As she opened her window slightly, she felt the cool morning breeze brush across her face, and she could smell the fresh air and the scents of the flowers outside. Penny also enjoyed reading her mystery books while she ate, but the book she started reading had a plot that entranced her so much she focused more on her book and what the characters did instead of eating her breakfast.

She brought her thoughts into captivity and realized that she needed to finish her breakfast so she could go to the bookstore and grocery store before it was time of lunch.

After Penny finished eating, she took her dishes to the sink and started rinsing them off so she could put them in the dishwasher and run it while she was out shopping. Then, she picked up her burgundy and white dishcloth and wiped off the white counter tops and stove so her kitchen would have a clean, orderly look in case any visitors came. When her stove and counter tops were cleaned, she closed her window and locked it, and then she walked back to her bedroom to get her purse and keys. As she walked into the living room and cautiously opened her door, she glanced up and down the hall to see if there was any activity. Since she didn't see anyone, she breathed a sigh of relief as she walked to the elevator.

She thought about her book that she finished reading. She liked how the author developed the plot and how the story ended. She liked the book so much that she was eager to purchase the next one in the series and some other cozies or crime fiction books that feature detectives.

The elevator arrived, and Penny was soon on her way down to the first floor. When the doors opened, she walked outside to her van, unlocked it, and climbed inside so she could go to the bookstore to look for some more mystery books in the series she started and some other mystery books.

Within a few minutes, Penny arrived at the shopping center and parked in the space right in front of the door to the bookstore. As she climbed out of her van, someone stopped her. "Are you Penny Marshall?"

Startled by the sound of her name, Penny turned to see who knew her and why the person stopped her. She saw a tall, slender, young looking man who had on blue trousers, light blue shirt, and brown shoes. "Do I know you?" Penny asked.

"I'm sorry I startled you. My name is Bob Wilson."

"How do you know me?"

"Isn't this you?" Bob asked, as he showed Penny her picture on the back of the book she wrote.

"Oh! That's my book! Yes, that's me," Penny said, as her eyes lit up.

"I thought so, but I wasn't sure because I noticed that you have changed your appearance."

"Have you read my book?"

"Not yet because I just bought it here at the bookstore, but it looks very intriguing," Bob said, with a smile.

"Thanks for your compliment. I enjoyed writing it, and I'm also working on my second book that I hope to have published soon."

"That's really great. I'd be happy to know when it's published and in the stores. I'd like to have a copy of it, too."

"Thank you for your interest in my books. I was just going into the bookstore so I could purchase another book in the series I just started reading because they're also intriguing, and I'm eager to get the second book."

"Would you autograph my book for me?"

"Sure," Penny replied, with a smile.

As Penny took out her pen to sign his book, the store manager saw them. "Aren't you Penny Marshall?" the manager asked her. She was average height, slender, and had short brown hair. Her green slacks and matching top enhanced her natural beauty.

"Yes," Penny replied.

"I'm Miss Jenkins. I'm the owner of Lakeview Bookstore. I saw you signing this book and wondered if you'd like to schedule a book signing in the store. I'd like to help you sell your book."

"Thanks. I'd like that very much."

"When are you available?"

"I'm not sure, but let me check my schedule." Penny opened up her small appointment book that she carried with her and checked the rest of the week. "I can be available tomorrow morning at 10:00 if that's all right?"

"That would be perfect for me. I'll have things ready for you by then. I just happened to have several copies of your book since it was recently published."

"Okay. I'll see you tomorrow morning," Penny replied.

"Great," Miss Jenkins said.

"That will be good for you to sign your books in the store," Bob replied.

"I know. I'm looking forward to it."

"Would you like to get something to eat?"

"I just finished eating breakfast a short time ago, so I'm really not hungry."

"I understand. How about something to drink? There's a little café right around the corner from here," Bob replied.

"Okay." *I guess it wouldn't hurt to go for a drink,* Penny thought to herself.

They walked around the corner and entered the cafe. Bob ordered a cup of coffee, and Penny ordered a medium Cherry Coke. Then, they sat down at a corner table and chatted.

"I like the coffee they serve here," Bob said, as he took a few sips.

"The Cherry Coke is good, too," Penny replied.

"I'm glad I ran into you today."

"Thanks. I'm looking forward to the book signing tomorrow because this is my first one since my book came out."

"That's good. I'm sure you'll sell a lot of books. I enjoy reading mysteries."

"I hope I can sell several, too because I could use the extra money right now."

"How long have you lived in Lakeview?"

"I just moved here Sunday."

"Oh. Where are you from?"

"California."

"That's a long way from here. What brought you to Lakeview?"

"I wanted a change in my life. I'm glad I moved here."

"I'm glad you moved here, too," Bob said, with a smile and a sparkle in his eyes.

"I should be going because I want to get some things ready before the book signing tomorrow."

"That's fine. I'm planning on coming tomorrow, too, if you don't mind."

"That's all right with me if you want to."

"Great," Bob replied. "I'll see you tomorrow," Bob said, as they walked out of the cafe.

"Okay."

Penny walked to her van and climbed inside. She wanted to go to the store to buy some good pens so she could have them for the book signing tomorrow. She drove around the shopping center and noticed that there was an office supply store in the same shopping center, so she parked in front of the building.

As she entered the store, she glanced around and saw where the pens were located. She walked down the aisle and chose some black pens that she thought would be easy to use. After that, she walked up and down the aisles to see if there was anything else she might need. Suddenly, she spotted the paper to make business cards.

"Business cards! I haven't thought about that. It would be a good idea to have business cards to advertise my freelance writing business and my books," Penny said to herself. As she browsed through the different packages, she found one that made thirty business cards to a page, so she picked up that package.

"Card stock! I could make some bookmarks for my business out of card stock. I think I'll get white." She also picked up a package of white card stock and then walked to the check out stand to pay for her purchases. Then, she walked outside to her van.

When Penny arrived at her apartment, she picked up her sack of office supplies and walked inside to the elevator. She pushed the button to the second floor, and when the elevator stopped, she stepped off and walked down the hall to her apartment. She unlocked her door and locked it after she entered her apartment, so nobody would intrude on her privacy. She walked over to her desk, set her package down, and turned on her computer so she could make her business cards and bookmarks.

As soon as her computer was ready, she sat down and called up her program that had business card formats. She found a design that she could use, but she just needed to redesign it so it would fit her needs. After she designed it with the right colors and design, she sat there and stared at the computer because she couldn't think of a name for her freelance writing business.

Finally, an idea popped into her head that she liked for her business name, so she typed it at the top of the card as well as a description of her services: freelance writer, copy editing, book reviews, column writing, eBooks, course developer, and article writing.

The last two things she needed were a design for her business logo and her phone number. As soon as her business card design was completed, she set it up for 30 to a page and printed it off on plain paper so she could view the design through her business card paper to make sure everything would fit. After that, she printed off the business cards. When she finished printing her business cards, she made her bookmarks that she wanted for her freelance writing. She used the same logo and information that was on her business cards so it would look more professional. As soon as everything was completed, she placed her cards and bookmarks inside a new larger folder so it would be ready for tomorrow morning.

Penny stood up and walked into the kitchen so she could see what she wanted for lunch because she was getting hungry. She opened the freezer section of her refrigerator and took out a TV dinner since it wouldn't take too long to cook. Then, she opened it up and put it into the microwave. Within five minutes, she took her dinner out of the microwave, took her silverware out of the drawer, and got a can of pop out of the refrigerator. After she walked into the living room, she set her plate on the coffee table in front of her and picked up the remote control to turn on the television. She continued to flip the channels until she found a mystery. Then, she sat on the sofa so she could watch television and eat.

When she finished eating, she walked into the kitchen to throw her trash away and wash her silverware. After she cleaned up her kitchen, she walked into the living room to watch her mystery show.

Later that night, she looked through her clothes to see what she wanted to wear to the book signing. She decided to wear her purple slacks, lavender blouse, and matching purple vest, so she put those together in a separate area away from her other clothes to remind her that she wanted to wear that outfit in the morning.

Penny walked into the kitchen to see what she wanted to eat for supper. She opened the refrigerator and took out a can of pop and the chicken salad mix so she could make a sandwich. Then, she took out her plate from the cupboard and walked into the living room to sit on the sofa to eat while she watched television.

After Penny ate, she started getting drowsy, so she took her things into the kitchen, and shut off the television. She walked into her bedroom to get ready for bed. Even though it was still early, she was eager to get up and prepare for her book signing.

Penny woke up when she sensed the early morning light shining in her bedroom window. She climbed out of bed to take a shower and wash her hair. After her shower, she dried her hair, put on her bathrobe, and walked into the kitchen to fix her some scrambled eggs and bacon. When it was ready, she sat on the sofa and watched television while she ate. The mystery intrigued her so much that when she glanced at the clock on her desk, she realized it was time for her to get ready to leave for her book signing. She quickly donned her clothes, picked up her envelope that contained her bookmarks and business cards, and her package of black pens. As soon as she had everything she needed, she walked out the door and locked it behind her. Soon she was on her way to the bookstore.

When she arrived, Miss Jenkins ushered Penny to a small table surrounded by her books, people were already glancing through her books.

After Penny sat down, she started signing the copies of her books for the customers. She felt like she was in a dream world because she couldn't believe she was sitting in the bookstore and signing her books. Penny's eyes gleamed as she signed each book because people were friendly and eager to meet her. As a result, Penny was glad she moved to Lakeview. She also liked Bob Wilson as a friend. However, she knew their relationship could never be anything more than a friendship. While Penny signed the books, Bob browsed around the mystery books section.

Two hours later, Penny finished signing the books, and the she stood up and stretched for a few minutes. She couldn't believe that she had solve several books.

"Hi, Penny," Bob said, as he approached her. "How did your book signing go today?"

"Great! I sold over twenty copies of my book."

"That's good. I bet you're happy with the royalties you made, too."

"Yes because I needed the extra money since I recently moved into a new apartment. By the way, here's a bookmark and my business card if you ever need my services."

"These look very professional. I'll keep them with me all the time, and I see they have your phone number," Bob said, as he glanced at the card and the bookmark.

"Thank you for the compliment. I just thought about making them last night since I was going to have the book signing."

"That was a great idea," Bob said, with a smile.

"Thanks. I need to be going, so I'll see you around."

"Okay. Can I call you sometime?"

"Sure, if you want, too," Penny replied. "I need to look for another book or two in the series I just started reading, so I'll talk to you later."

"Okay. I hope I can see you again," Bob said, with a smile.

When Bob left, Penny walked over to the mystery section and noticed that the next two books in the series were available, so she picked up the books. She was excited about the two books and was eager to start reading them. She walked up to the checkout stand and paid for them. Then, she walked out the door, climbed into her van, and on her way back to her apartment, she thought about the day. *I can't believe I had my first book signing. That was so thrilling to me.*

Now, I want to write my next book and get it published so people will buy it, too.

Penny parked in front of the building, picked up her books, climbed out of the van, and locked it. Then she entered the building and walked to the elevator.

After Penny unlocked her door, she walked inside, and shut her door. She put her package on the table beside the sofa. She breathed a sigh of relief, and then her stomach growled, so she walked cheerfully into the kitchen to fix her some lunch. She browsed through the refrigerator and chose a TV dinner since it wouldn't take that long to cook. She wanted to spend less time cooking so she could read her book sooner.

While her dinner cook, she opened her silverware drawer and took out a fork and spoon. She also took out a can of pop from the refrigerator. After that, her dinner finished cooking, so she took it out of the oven and placed it on a plate. Then, she walked into the living room so she could settle down on her sofa to eat and watch television, but she was too excited to sit down. She stood up and started dancing and singing around the room because she sold several books today at the book signing.

Finally, Penny calmed down and finished eating her lunch and took her things to the kitchen and cleaned it up. After that, she sat down on the sofa and tried to read her book, but she had trouble concentrating because of the events that happened today in her life. However, she managed to take her thoughts captive for a short time, but her thoughts flooded her mind again. *I'm glad I had the book signing and sold that many books. That was a miracle because I hadn't even thought of a book signing.*

Bookstore! Book! Now I know how people are recognizing me. Why didn't I think of that before? I hope nobody is here from

California because I don't want anyone to recognize me. Wait a minute! The man who called me Susan Salters? He must have come from California. How did he know I was here? I've got to find out who he is, but how? I don't want to run into him again.

Penny focused again on her book. She was intrigued with this story, too, so she was glad she went to the bookstore. A few minutes later, Penny starting thinking about Bob. *He seems like a nice person, but the relationship can't be anything more than a friendship. I don't know what I'd tell him if he asked me out. I'm not sure I'd feel comfortable going out with him or any guy until my problems are resolved in California.*

Chapter Four
Penny's Date

Early Wednesday morning, Penny crawled out of bed so she could take her shower and get dressed. After she donned her purple slacks, lavender short-sleeved blouse, and matching purple sweater, she put on her sock and athletic shoes and walked into the kitchen to cook her breakfast, which consisted of bacon and biscuits. She also poured some orange juice in a yellow plastic glass and walked into the living room to watch television while she ate. Watching television helped Penny to relax and forget about her struggles in California at least temporarily.

She thought about Bob and how she liked him, but she acknowledged the fact that her relationship with Bob could only be a friendship. Even though Penny wanted her past relationships to work out and didn't want to leave, she was too upset because of what happened and knew she had to escape so she could start a new life far away to give her time to think about a resolution to her problems.

Penny became startled when the phone rang because she couldn't imagine who would be calling her this early in the morning. Then, she thought about Bob and wondered if it could be him, or maybe someone from the book signing who had her card and bookmark. She picked up the phone and answered. "Hello."

"Penny, this is Bob. How are you this morning?"

"I'm fine. I'm still amazed that I had my first book signing yesterday."

"Now, I know a published author in person."

"Thanks," Penny said.

"I'd like to see you again sometime soon."

Penny hesitated for a few minutes because she didn't know what to say. She liked Bob, but she didn't know what to do about going out with him.

"Penny. Are you there?"

"Yes. I was just thinking about something." *Maybe it would be all right since I'm far away from California. It's not likely that someone would see me with him. Unless...*

"Would you like to go out for supper tonight?"

"Let me check my schedule." Penny hesitated a few minutes, and then she finally told him that she would accept his invitation for supper.

"Great. I'll pick you up around 5:00."

"Okay."

After Penny hung up, she walked into the kitchen, washed her dishes, and cleaned up the counter tops. She always liked to keep her apartment clean and organized because she grew up in an environment where she had to be perfect, or she would have to suffer the consequences if she made a mistake.

When her kitchen was spotless, she walked into the living room and placed her papers in her file cabinet, dusted the furniture, and walked into her bedroom with her books and set them on the bedside table so she could have them handy before she went to sleep. Penny always liked to read a chapter or two in her mystery books or write in her journal before going to bed. Then, she walked into the living room and turned on the television until 4:30. While she listened to the television, she used her convenient vacuum for everyday touch up cleaning, and then once a week, she would bring out her larger sweeper to clean it up more, so she was glad that she brought both sweepers with her from California.

After she looked around her apartment and was satisfied with the way it looked, she realized Bob didn't have her address, and she didn't have his phone number, so she didn't know what was going to happen.

Within a few minutes, the phone rang again. "Penny, hi, it's me, Bob. I just realized I don't have your address."

"I know. I realized it, too." She gave him the address, and then she hung up.

Around 5:00, Penny heard a knock on the door. As she opened the door, Bob came inside. "Hi, Penny. Are you ready?"

"Yes."

"Great! Where would you like to go?"

"I like Mexican food the best, but wherever you'd like to go is fine with me," Penny replied.

"So do I, and I know a great Mexican restaurant that I'm sure you'll enjoy."

"That sounds good to me. I'm looking forward to eating Mexican food because I haven't had it for several days."

"You'll like this place," Bob said, with a smile.

Penny followed Bob out the door and locked it. When they were outside, he opened up her door so she could climb inside, and then he walked around to his side of the car and climbed in. Soon, they were on their way to the restaurant.

"By the way, who made the business cards and bookmarks?" Bob asked.

"I did. I have a color printer and the programs that have formats for the business cards and bookmarks. All I needed to buy was the paper."

"That's amazing. You did a great job on those because they look professional," Bob commented.

"Thanks," Penny replied, with a smile.

"We're here," Bob said.

After Bob parked the car, he walked around to Penny's side and opened the door. Then, they walked to the door of the restaurant, and Bob opened the door so Penny could enter first.

"Good afternoon. Welcome to *South of the Border*. Will this be dine-in or to go?" A young looking woman asked, as she greeted them with a smile.

"Dine-in," Bob replied.

"Smoking or Non-Smoking?"

"Non-Smoking, please," Bob replied.

"Follow me."

The hostess led them to a booth in a quiet corner. "Is this all right?"

"Yes," Bob said. "This is perfect. Thank you."

They sat down, and the hostess gave them their menus.

"What would you like to drink while you're looking at the menus?"

"Cherry Coke," Penny replied.

"Same for me," Bob said.

They looked through the menus to decide what they wanted. Penny chose Beef Sanchos with rice and beans, and then she ordered a small dinner salad. Bob ordered the same thing.

"What do you think of this place?" Bob asked.

"It seems like a nice place. The decorations enhance the name of the restaurant," Penny commented.

"The pictures and the wallpaper do enhance the name, and the food is just as great. That's why I enjoy eating here."

Within a few minutes, the waitress brought chips and salsa that came with their meal. "Here's some chips and salsa for your appetizer, and I'll bring the food to you shortly."

"That's fine," Bob said.

"The chips and salsa are great," Penny commented, as she took a bite of chips and salsa.

"I like them, too. I also take a bag of chips and some salsa home for snacks."

"That sounds good to me, too. I do have some extra money for some snacks, so I might do that, too."

"Don't worry about that because I planned on treating you to anything you would like to eat here or to take home for snacks," Bob replied.

"Oh," Penny said, as her mind started to wonder back to California and the home she left. She continued to think about her life, as she picked up a chip and dipped it into the salsa.

Someone approached their table and told Penny hi, but she didn't hear the person. Finally, Bob spoke up. "Penny, are you all right?"

Startled, Penny said, "Yes." Then, she noticed Abby.

"Hi Penny."

"Hi."

"How are you?" Abby asked.

"Okay," Penny replied, as she ate her chip and salsa.

"Hi Bob. How are you doing?"

"I'm doing fine. How about you?"

"Great. I'll talk to you later because I don't want to intrude on your supper," Abby said.

"That's fine. I'll see you later," Bob replied.

"See you, Penny," Abby said.

"Okay," Penny replied, as she ate another chip. *Why do I keep running into her? I hope I don't see her again because I'm still mad at her for bumping into my car.*

"Are you all right?" Bob asked Penny. "You seem like you're off in another world."

"I'm sorry, but my mind seems to wander at times. I'm fine," Penny replied. "I'm still a little upset because she bumped into my car."

"I can understand, but Abby is a nice person, so I hope you two can work out your problems."

"Maybe."

As the waitress returned with the food, Penny looked at her plate and couldn't believe the amount of food.

"Wow! I'm amazed at the amount of food they serve here. I hope I can eat it all," she said, when the waitress left.

"They do serve large portions, but they have containers so you can take food home if you don't eat it all here. I do that sometimes, and I also order extra chips and salsa to take home for later."

"That's good because I may have to take some of this home for later."

They were so involved with their meal they didn't converse that much. After Penny ate about half of her food, she told Bob that she wanted to take the rest home.

When the waitress came to check on them, Bob told her they needed a couple of take home containers as well as two bags of chips and two orders of salsa to take home. "Okay. I'll be back shortly."

Within ten minutes, the waitress returned to their table with their containers, and the chips and salsa. They also paid the waitress for their meal.

"Thanks for lunch," Penny said, as they walked out the door.

"You're welcome."

Soon, they were on their way back to Penny's apartment.

When they arrived, Bob parked in the guest parking space, opened the door for Penny, and then opened the entrance to the apartment building.

They arrived at Penny's door, and as Penny unlocked the door and opened it, she thanked Bob for the supper. "Thanks for supper and the snacks. I had a good time."

"You're welcome. I enjoyed our time together, too, and I'd like to take you out again."

"I'll have to see," Penny replied, with a smile. "Right now, I have to get some writing done because I'm working on my next book."

"That's fine. I don't want to force myself on you, so I'll talk to you later."

"Thanks for understanding."

Bob left, and Penny walked inside and locked her door. She put her purse and keys in her bedroom, and then she walked into the kitchen to place her salsa inside the refrigerator and the chips in a plastic covered container on the counter. She was glad that she had some chips and salsa because she wanted snacks while she read.

After that, she sat on the sofa and thought about Bob. *I enjoy being with Bob because he seems like a nice person, but it can only be a friendship. It has to be that way with any guy I meet.* Penny turned on the television and clicked from station to station until she found a mystery that looked intriguing. She couldn't believe what she was watching. It was about a young couple who met and started dating.

The girl had some kind of secret that she kept hidden from the guy, and when the guy found out the secret, he became upset with the girl. He felt deceived and wanted to get even with her. As a result, the girl became afraid of what the guy might do, so she decided to leave for a few days because she didn't want him to locate her. She felt if she left, he might forget about her and turn to someone else, so the girl decided to go camping.

Camping! That's what I'd like to do.

Penny shut off the television, gathered up some snacks, and put them in her cooler. Then, she put some of her clothes inside a bag and took her laptop and a few accessories. After she picked up her purse, keys, cooler, and bag, she opened the door and walked into the hall. Then, she locked the door and hurried downstairs to her van. She opened the back door and put her things inside and then climbed into the van and headed for the campsite where she stayed Sunday night.

When she arrived, she unlocked the door to her trailer and climbed inside so she could stay hidden for a few days. She put her things down and relaxed on her bed that was inside.

Chapter Five

Crimewriter's E-mail

Early Thursday morning, Penny put on her brown slacks, beige blouse, her socks, and athletic shoes. She ate a strawberry yogurt and then grabbed her brown sweater and walked outside. As she looked around the campsite, she noticed the oak and cedar trees that surrounded her area. Since she felt a cool breeze, she put on her sweater.

While she walked, she noticed another car and camper nearby, so she cautiously walked passed the area because nobody would see her. Penny couldn't believe she saw Abby again. She quickly hid among the bushes and trees so Abby wouldn't spot her.

After Penny waited for a few minutes, she realized that she was safe. Penny stood up and walked back towards her van and trailer. She knew she had to leave, so she hooked up her trailer to the back of her van and made sure she locked her trailer as well as her van. She climbed into her van and drove east towards her apartment.

She thought about going to a shopping center because she liked the one near her apartment building, but she wasn't eager to return there. Since too many people claimed they knew her, Penny wasn't sure where she would go next.

Penny continued to drive east until she saw another shopping center. She parked her car in a parking space in front of a Super Mart. She liked Super Mart because it had almost everything she needed in one place. After she walked inside, she took a cart out of the rack and started to walk down the aisle with the fresh fruits and vegetables.

As Penny walked down an aisle, she looked at the prices. She couldn't believe the prices because they were cheaper than other places. She also liked the store because the floors were clean and the shelves were organized. She picked up some chicken tenders, fish sticks, pizza, frozen potatoes, and frozen vegetables. Then, she walked down the next aisle and picked up some cranberry sauce, applesauce, peaches, and crushed pineapple. At the end of that aisle, there were containers for the fresh meats. She picked up some hamburger and chicken fried steak patties. After that, she remembered she needed some personal items, so she walked down the aisle that had the paper products and picked up some bath tissue, paper towels, Kleenex, and some air fresheners. She had all of the items she needed, so she walked to a check out stand. Nobody was ahead of her, so she started placing her groceries on the counter, but as she glanced at the clerk, she looked away immediately.

Penny thought, *How did she get here so fast? Maybe it wasn't Abby I saw at the campground.* She avoided eye contact with her, and when she had her groceries sacked and paid for, she quickly hurried out the door to her car.

"Oh no! I can't believe it. I'm glad she didn't notice me. On the other hand, maybe she did notice me but didn't recognize me."

Penny put her groceries in her van and drove back to her apartment. "I guess I won't be going there again." Penny said to herself.

When she arrived at her apartment, she grabbed her sacks and rushed inside. She pushed the button to the elevator to go upstairs, and within a few seconds, Penny got off the elevator and walked down the hall to her apartment.

She unlocked the door and walked inside. Then, she shut the door and locked it. Penny breathed a sigh of relief as she set her groceries on the kitchen table. Penny was glad to be back inside her apartment where she felt safe.

After she had her groceries put away, she walked into the living room and sat on the sofa to relax. She picked up her TV remote control, turned on the television, and flipped the stations until she found a mystery movie. Penny enjoyed watching mysteries because she liked writing them. As she watched the movie, she felt her body tense up because she felt like she was right there with the main character. When Penny saw someone following the main character on the show, she became startled by the sound of a knock on her own door. She trembled all over as fear started to swell up inside.

She calmed down after she thought it might be Mr. Martin. Penny opened the door and stared at the slender looking woman with long blonde hair. "Can I help you?" Penny asked nonchalantly.

"Hi. I'm Abby Fisher. I just got off work and came home. I live in Apartment 215 and knew that you lived here, so I wanted to come and see you."

Abby was the same size and weight as Penny, and they both wore casual clothes because they wanted to be comfortable. However, they still wanted to look professional since they worked at home.

"Oh," Penny replied.

"Is everything all right? You seemed a little nervous when you opened the door."

"Oh. I thought you were Mr. Martin. He's the only one who knows I live here."

"I'm sorry about the accident, and I hope we can be friends," Abby said.

"That's all right. I'm sorry I stopped in the middle of the street."

"If you want to talk, I live in apartment 215."

"Okay," Penny replied.

Abby turned and left, and Penny shut the door. *Why do I keep bumping into her? Maybe I'll write to Crimesolver and see how she's doing.*

Crimewriter's E-mail Letter

"Hi, Crimesolver. How are you today? I finally have my own apartment, and I like it here. How's your case coming? Things are going better for me even though some strange things have happened to me since I moved here. Someday I'll tell you about it. Tomorrow, I'm going to put up some signs to advertise my freelance writing service. By the way, I went to a bookstore in this nearby shopping center, and I got to see my first book that I had published. It was fun seeing my name in print and in the bookstore. I also had a book signing, and that was exciting. I made business cards and bookmarks for my freelance writing business.

Crimesolver's E-mail Letter

"Hi, Crimewriter. I'm doing fine. It's been a strange few days, but everything is all right. I just had a fender bender the other day. I bumped into a woman who stopped in the middle of the street. I thought she was going to turn into the shopping center, but she didn't, and she became angry at me, but it's all right. I even paid for her gas

and for her repairs on her van. I hope someday I can be friends with her because she seems like a nice person, and she's about my age.

Oh well, enough of that. I hope you're happy in your new apartment. Bye for now.

Penny was shocked at what she read. "It couldn't be her! Now what do I do?"

Chapter Six
Penny Meets Crimesolver

When Penny woke up Friday morning, she took her shower and put on her brown slacks, beige blouse, her brown vest, and her socks and shoes. As she entered the kitchen, she started to fix some eggs, but was interrupted when she heard a knock on the door. She peeked through the peephole and saw Abby standing there. *I guess I'll let her inside. From her e-mail letters, she seemed like a nice person.* Penny thought, as she opened the door.

"Hi, Penny."

"Hi. I was about to fix some breakfast. Would you like to eat with me?"

"I'd like that, if you're sure you want me to stay and eat with you because I don't want to impose on you," Abby replied, with a surprised look on her face.

"I'd be happy to have you eat with me, and I want to apologize for the way I've acted toward you."

"That's all right," Abby replied, as she sat down at the kitchen table.

"Thanks for understanding," Penny said.

"I'm glad we're getting together because I really wanted to spend time with you since we're about the same age."

"We have something to talk about, so I'm glad you came over," Penny said, as she placed the scrambled eggs, bacon, biscuits, and orange juice on the table.

"What?" Abby asked.

As Penny took out the plates, silverware, and glasses she told Abby about the e-mail she received. "I received an e-mail last night that shocked me."

"What was it, if you don't mind sharing?"

"I've been writing e-mail letters to someone I haven't met. We've had a great time writing to each other, and it was easier for me to meet people on the Internet than in person."

"That's neat," Abby interrupted. "I've been writing to someone, too, whom I really like even though we haven't met."

"I found out who my e-mail friend was and where she lived. We've been using different names because we didn't want to give out our real names, but God must have wanted me to find out the identity of my e-mail friend."

"Who is the person?"

"You," Penny replied, as she showed Crimesolver the e-mail letter.

"Are you serious? You're crimewriter!" Abby exclaimed.

"I never dreamed we'd meet either," Penny replied.

"How long have you lived here?" Abby asked.

"I moved to Lakeview on Sunday, and then I found this apartment complex on Monday," Penny replied.

"That's great because I live down the hall from you. Where are you from?"

"California."

"That's a long way from here," Abby commented. "What brought you here to Lakeview?"

"I wanted to move here because I needed a change in my life. Where are you from?" Penny quickly changed the subject because she didn't want to reveal why she left California.

"Lakeview. I've lived here all of my life, but I moved into this apartment complex two years ago because I wanted an apartment instead of a duplex."

"I like it here, too. Mr. Martin seems like a nice manager," Penny replied.

"He's been very helpful to me when I first moved in to this apartment."

"He's been good to me, too."

"Besides solving crimes as an amateur detective, I work part time in a grocery store," Abby said.

"I know because I saw you the other day when I was in there."

"I'm glad we could finally meet," Abby said, with a smile.

"I am, too."

"We have a lot in common," Abby said.

"We sure do," Penny said. "God must have wanted me to move here so we could meet."

"I have an idea. Would you like to work together?"

"How would we do that since I'm a freelance writer, and you're an amateur detective?" Penny asked.

"I've always wanted to be a writer, and you could show me how," Abby said.

"That sounds good to me because I've had a desire to solve crimes as an amateur detective, and I've wanted to start a mystery reader's book club."

"That sounds like a great idea. We might even solve real crimes in our book club," Abby suggested.

"That's super. I know I'm going to enjoy working together with you," Penny commented, with a smile.

"Me, too," Abby replied.

"By the way, I'm sorry about the other day and causing the accident," Penny said.

"That's all right. I'm glad we're friends now."

"Me, too."

After Penny and Abby ate breakfast, they sat on the sofa and discussed freelance writing, developing a mystery reader's book club, and being amateur detectives. They were glad that they met and would be working together. Since both girls enjoyed reading and writing mysteries, they were eager to start their mystery book club.

"How are we going to work together?" Abby asked.

"I thought we could spend some time together a few mornings a week to work on writing, and then in the afternoons and weekends, we could go our separate ways so we could have our privacy and work on the projects that we've taken," Penny suggested.

"That sounds reasonable to me," Abby agreed. "I like my privacy sometimes, too."

They decided to work together on Monday and Wednesday mornings in Abby's apartment and Tuesday and Thursday mornings in Penny's apartment. They wanted to have their mystery reader's book club on Friday morning and work the rest of the time on their own unless they had a project where they had to work together.

The first thing that Penny and Abby wanted to do was to make some flyers for their freelance writing so they could post them in different stores and on the bulletin board in the main entrance of their apartment building.

Then, when someone contacted them about writing jobs, they divided the assignments according to their abilities and interests.

Since today was Friday, they decided to start their mystery reader's book club, but they chose to work in Abby's apartment today. Penny did the dishes and put them away. Then, she walked into her bedroom to get the mystery book that she started reading, her laptop, and other accessories that she needed to have for writing and their book club.

Abby opened the door and walked out while Penny followed behind and locked her door. They walked down the hall to Abby's apartment, and Abby opened the door. They walked inside, and Abby had Penny set her work on the rectangular kitchen table so they could work together.

"You have a nice color scheme here," Penny commented. "I like the cream-colored walls with the purple curtains that hang over your white blinds and the lavender carpet in your living room."

"Thanks. I like it here, too, and I like the color scheme in your apartment. By the way, do you have any writing projects that you're working on now?" Abby asked.

"Not yet. Since I just moved to Lakeview, I haven't had a chance to advertise my freelance writing service."

"Mr. Martin will let us put up an announcement on the bulletin board in the main entrance and on the bulletin board on the second floor," Abby said.

"That sounds good to me. Do you have anything that we can use to make flyers?"

"Yes. I do have some poster paper that we can use. It's in my bedroom, so I'll get it."

Abby walked into her bedroom to search for the poster paper and markers that they could use to make the flyers. After she located them, she walked back into the kitchen and placed them on the kitchen table.

"The white poster paper will work out great, and so will the markers," Penny commented.

"I thought they would, too," Abby replied. "I'm excited about making the posters, so we could start our freelance writing."

They started working on their flyers so they could post them on the bulletin boards in their apartment complex. When they completed their flyers, they walked downstairs and put them on the bulletin boards on the first floor, and on the bulletin board on the second floor. After that, they walked back to Abby's apartment and sat on the sofa to discuss their book club.

Penny showed Abby her new mystery book that she bought. She told Abby about the book, and they decided to start reading it. Since it was the second book in the series, Abby decided to get the first book and the second book, so she would have a better understanding of the series. However, they still wanted to talk about some elements of fiction so they will have a better understanding of mysteries.

"Have you read many mystery books?" Penny asked Abby.

"I've read some, but I mainly read crime fiction because that feature amateur detectives since I work as an amateur detective."

"This will be great because we can help each other reach their goals in reading and understanding mysteries as well as solving crimes," Penny replied. "Let's talk about the elements of fiction, so we can get started before we read."

"Okay."

"First, the elements are themes, characters, plots, and settings. A theme is the main idea of the story. It's what the writer wants to reveal to readers."

"Yes," Abby agreed.

"The characters in a mystery are the protagonists, villains, and suspects."

"Right. Protagonists are usually the detective, but they can be villains."

"I agree. I've read some stories where the narrator was the villain, and those are interesting stories, too," Abby said. "I also enjoy reading mysteries that seem to have impossible crimes or locked room mysteries. Those are intriguing to me."

"I enjoy reading those kinds of stories, too. Stories can be character-driven or plot-driven. In character-driven stories, the characters change because of their circumstances. The characters have some problem they experience, and they have to decide which way to go. In plot-driven stories, the characters don't change. The focus is on the plot instead of the characters."

"I understand," Abby said.

"Settings are where the story takes place. Settings can be anywhere depending on the type of crime fiction the writer wants to create."

"Thanks for explaining the elements. This will help to understand what I'm reading," Abby commented.

"You're welcome. It has helped me. When we read, we can focus on how the detectives solve their cases, and then we can learn to apply their techniques in solving cases to the cases we have as amateur detectives."

"That's right. Let's focus on what the amateur detective does in the book and talk about that next Friday."

"That will be interesting because we'll learn how to investigate our own cases," Penny said.

"True."

After that, they decided to meet next Friday and discuss the book and look at how the amateur detective investigated a case and gathered clues so she could solve it.

An hour later, the phone rang and Abby answered it. When she hung up, she told Penny about the assignment. "We just received a writing assignment."

"Super," Penny said.

"The person is Annie Salyers, and she said she lives in this apartment complex just down the hall from me."

"That will be good," Penny replied.

The phone rang again, and after Abby hung up, she told Penny they had another writing job from someone named Callie Green. She told Penny that both of them would drop their manuscripts by in a few minutes, and they would like their assignments completed as soon as possible."

"Sounds good to me."

"One is a book review. Since I've already read the book, I can do that one. The other one is a copy editing assignment, which is a cover letter that she wrote to a publisher and wants us to proofread and edit before she sends it to him."

"That would be fine with me," Penny replied. Penny liked the copy editing assignment because she had a degree in English with a writing emphasis, and she liked helping people polish their material.

When Abby heard a knock on the door, she got up and answered it. "Hi, I'm Callie Green. Are you Abby?"

"Yes."

"Here's my manuscript that I'd like you to proofread and edit."

"Thank you. A friend of mine, Penny, also started working with me, so I'm giving this project to her. Penny is a freelance writer, and she's helping me to get started."

"That's nice that you two can work together," Callie said, as she turned to walk back down the hall to her apartment.

Just as Abby was about to sit down, she heard another knock on the door, so she walked to the door and answered it. "Are you Abby Fisher?"

"Yes."

"I'm Annie Salyers. Here's my book and the rough draft of my book review and a copy of my book. I'd appreciate it if you could rewrite the book review and type it in a professional manner."

"That's fine. I'll have it done this week. Penny and I are working together as freelance writers and amateur sleuths."

"That's nice. I'll see you later."

Abby closed the door and locked it, and then they decided to sit down at the kitchen table so they could start working on their assignments. As they sat there quietly and worked, they listened to the birds chirping outside the slightly opened window. "Listening to the birds help me relax," Abby said.

"That helps me, too as well as the gentle spring breeze blowing in through the window. Springtime is so peaceful, especially in the early morning or early evening."

"I hadn't thought about that before, but I like having my window open some so I can feel the spring breeze. By the way, what kinds of things do you enjoy doing?" Abby asked.

"I enjoy camping because I can be alone and ponder my circumstances. I also like watching the sunset sparkle on the water."

"That sounds like fun. I enjoy camping, too, but I don't like getting bit by insects."

"I don't either. That's why I take my bug spray with me because it helps keep bugs from biting me," Penny said.

"That's a good idea. I'll have to get something to keep the bugs from biting me before I go camping."

"I also use sun tan lotion because I don't want to get a sun burn," Penny said.

"I can't be exposed to too much sun either."

"We've been chatting for awhile, so I guess we need to get back to work," Penny said, with a smile.

"True."

They started working on their writing, and when they were finished, they walked into the living room and sat on the sofa. "That was fun working together. I'm glad you came over to my apartment," Penny said.

"I am, too."

"I need to leave now because I have a few errands to run today plus I want to write in my journal. I have some private places in my computer where I write down things I don't want others to see," Penny said.

"That's good. I enjoy working on the computer, too. I've also started writing a journal because I've found it has helped me to write down things that happen in my life. I can also look back and see what I did and how I felt about what happened."

"It does help," Penny agreed, as she stood up and walked towards the door. "I'll see you Monday."

"Okay. Have a good day."

Penny opened the door and walked quickly down the hall to her apartment because she still didn't want anyone to recognize her.

She unlocked her door, put her laptop and accessories on her desk in the living room, and then walked into the kitchen to fix some lunch. She opened her freezer and noticed she had chicken nuggets and frozen roasted potatoes, so she took the packages out and placed some of the chicken nuggets on a small cookie sheet and potatoes on another one. After she turned on the oven, she put the cookie sheets inside and set the timer so she wouldn't forget about her food this time because she has forgotten about things in the past. While her food cooked, she took out her white plate with light blue and yellow flowers, silverware, and blue plastic glass and set them on the table. When the timer went off on the stove, Penny took her food out of the oven and placed several chicken nuggest and potates on the plate and sat down to eat.

As Penny ate, she thought about her plans for the afternoon. *I need to look for a boat that I can leave at a campsite so it will be available when I go camping.* After that, she decided to make a list of things she needed, so she took out a 3 x 5 card and started writing out her list so she wouldn't forget anything.

As soon as Penny made out her list and finished eating, she cleaned up the kitchen. Then, she picked up her purse and keys and walked out the door. She locked it and then walked to the elevator.

While she waited for the elevator, she thought about the guy she met the first day and was glad she hadn't seen him again. She hoped she wouldn't because he looked familiar, but she didn't know who he was.

When she arrived on the first floor, she walked out to her van. She liked going to Super Mart because she could find furniture, small appliances, office supplies, clothes, food, and other items that she needed instead of going to several stores.

Penny found another Super Mart, which was two miles north of her apartment complex. After she locked up her van, she walked inside the store and got a cart for her groceries. She found some canned goods, boxed dinners, tuna, macaroni and cheese, two cartons of pop, potato chips, TV dinners, fish sticks, popcorn shrimp, graham crackers, and some frozen chicken nuggets. She also found another tablecloth for her kitchen table that would blend in with the color scheme in her kitchen, and then she walked down the aisle to purchase some office supplies that she needed for her desktop computer.

When she picked up her groceries and other supplies, she walked to a check out area that didn't have anyone in line and paid for her things. She walked outside to her van and unlocked the side of it so she could put her purchases inside. Then, she drove back to her apartment.

Just as Penny pulled into her parking space, she saw Mr. Martin standing outside. She opened the van door and climbed out.

"Hi, Mr. Martin."

"Hi, Miss Marshall. How are you today?"

"I'm fine. I went to Super Mart and picked up a few things that I needed."

"Do you need any help unloading your van?"

"No thank you. I don't have many sacks."

Penny took out a couple of sacks and walked inside to her apartment. She opened her door and put her groceries away. After that, she walked outside to her van so she could carry the other belongings inside.

As Penny put her purchases away, she thought about her plans for Saturday. She wanted to check out the other campsites because she wanted to see which one she preferred because she wasn't that interested in the one west of her place, so she hoped the one north or east of her apartment would be a better campsite. She also wanted to find a nice secluded area for her trailer.

Once Penny had her groceries put away, she walked into the living room and turned on her television to see if there was a good mystery show on. She found one she liked, so she sat on the sofa to watch her movie. As she watched the movie, she thought about what she wanted to eat for supper. She decided to do something different, so she ordered a pizza. She called up the nearest pizza place and ordered a pizza that she could have delivered. Within an hour, her pizza arrived, and she set it on the kitchen table. She took out a plate and placed a couple of slices on it. Then, she opened the refrigerator, took out a can of pop, and walked into the living room. She sat on the sofa and ate her pizza as she watched television.

After she ate the two slices, she put the rest of the pizza away for the next day. Penny walked into the bathroom, took a shower, and shampooed her hair.

Then, she put on her blue flowered pajamas and walked into the living room, so she could turn off her television and lights. After that, she walked into her bedroom and picked up her journal, which she kept on her bedside table, and turned to the next blank page. She started writing down her thoughts.

Crimewriter's Journal

I'm glad I moved into this apartment complex, and I'm glad Abby came over this morning because it was good to meet Crimesolver. I know we're going to enjoy working together on writing, solving crimes, and our book club. However, I still have to be careful because there have been people who seem to know me, so it's difficult for me to trust too many people right now.

After Penny finished writing in her journal, she put it on the lamp table and shut off her light. Then, she dozed off to sleep.

Chapter Seven
The Campgrounds

Penny woke up early Saturday morning so she could check out the campgrounds. She climbed out of bed, took a shower put on her green slacks, white blouse, green sweater, socks, and shoes. As soon as she was dressed, she put on her new wig. *I wonder if Abby will recognize me in my new wig because it does make me look different. The color is darker, and it's curlier than my own hair, but I guess I'll find out when I see her on Monday.*

Penny walked into the kitchen and took out a breakfast TV dinner because she liked cooking things that were easy. She wanted to spend most of her time writing and working on her computer since she just started developing her own website to advertise her freelance writing. She sat down to eat her breakfast and drink her orange juice.

Then, she cleaned up the kitchen and walked into the living room. Just as she sat on the sofa, she heard a knock on the door. She stood up and opened the door and saw Abby standing there.

"I'm sorry I must have the wrong apartment. I was looking for Penny Marshall." Abby said, as she looked at the number on the door.

"Hi, Abby."

"Do I know you?" Abby asked, curiously.

"I'm Penny."

"Wow! I didn't recognize you because you look so different," Abby said, with a surprised look.

"I have a wig on."

"I like it. You really look different with the wig."

"Thanks. I wanted a different appearance, so I bought a couple of wigs."

Penny was glad that Abby didn't recognize her, so she knew her plan worked. "How are you doing?"

"I'm all right. How about yourself?" Abby asked.

"I'm fine."

"I had a few more phone calls for writing jobs this morning, so I wanted to let you know now instead of waiting until Monday," Abby said.

"Our freelance writing is starting to build because I have three jobs for each us, and they didn't care which one of us did the work."

"That's great because I could use the extra money right now," Penny replied.

"I know what you mean. I need some extra money, too."

"What kind of writing jobs are they?" Penny asked

"I have two book reviews for mystery books, two assignments for short stories for children, and two article assignments about freelance writing and earning a living. I thought I would give you one of each, and I would take one of each."

"That sounds good to me. When are these assignments due?"

"The book reviews are due by next Friday, so we have time to do them, but the other assignments are due Wednesday."

"That will work out for me," Penny replied. "We could get together now if you want to. I needed to run some errands, but I could do that after we work together."

"Okay," Abby replied.

"Let's work at the kitchen table," Penny suggested.

"I'd like to visit about freelance writing before we actually get together and write," Abby said.

"That sounds good to me."

"Where do you get your ideas?" Abby asked.

"I get ideas from just about anywhere. When I watch television or read mystery books, I'm open to ideas that may arise. I also observe people while I'm shopping, or when I'm talking to people on the phone or in person, I listen to what they're saying. Sometimes I come up with some great plot ideas, character names, themes, and settings."

"Those are great ideas. I didn't know where writers got their ideas for stories and books."

"I keep a journal of my story ideas beside my bed so I can be ready with something when someone calls me. All I have to do is to look through my journal and see if there's something I can use," Penny said. "I also have a writing folder on my computer where I can put my ideas.

"This is super. I'll have to start doing that."

"You can also write about your personal experiences. All you have to do is to fictionalize your stories or articles so you aren't using real names and end up offending someone," Penny said.

"How long have you been a freelance writer?"

"Four years. How long have you been an amateur detective?"

"Two years. It's an exciting and rewarding job because I'm helping people solve their cases. I also enjoy solving helping the police detectives when I can."

"That's neat."

"When did you get your first book published?" Abby asked.

"Last month."

"What kind of book is it?" Abby asked.

"It's a mystery, and now I'm getting royalties," Penny said, with a smile.

"That's good."

"It seems like we have a lot in common," Penny commented.

"That's true."

When it was time for lunch, Abby told Penny she would see her on Monday, and that she was looking forward to working on their projects together and critiquing each other's work. Penny agreed that it would be fun working together because she thought they'd get more business if there were two of them.

Abby gathered up her supplies and walked toward the door. Penny opened the door and walked into the hall with Abby. "I hope you have a good day," Penny said.

"Thanks. I hope you do, too," Abby said.

Penny walked back inside and picked up her purse and keys because she wanted to check out the campsites. She opened her door and walked into the hall. As she looked toward the elevator, she saw someone she thought looked familiar, so she closed her door since she didn't want to see anyone from California.

Then, she thought she might be mistaken. "It seems like everyone I see looks familiar to me, but I don't see how that's possible because nobody from California would know I moved to Lakeview. I don't see how they could unless..."

Penny waited for a few minutes, and then she walked toward the elevator and pushed the button. Within a few seconds, she was on her way down to the first floor.

She walked out the main entrance to her van and unlocked it so she could climb inside. She drove around for a few minutes, and then she decided to check out the other campsites, so she headed east to look at the campsite. Within a half hour, she arrived at the campsite. She saw several oak trees surrounding the campsite and roads that led to different areas of the campground. She drove down one of the roads that led to a secluded area and saw where she could park her van and trailer. As she looked around the area, she spotted the lake, but she wondered what the name of this campsite was, so she looked around for the name. She finally saw the sign that had Pine Oaks Campsite printed in black letters on a white board. Penny thought this campsite was all right, but she wanted to check out the other one. After she left, she headed north to the other one.

Within thirty minutes, she arrived at the campsite and saw the name, Lake Oakwood Campsite printed in brown letters on an attractive tan colored board that had oak trees in the corners. She also saw a secluded area and a building where she could keep her trailer. It seemed like there were more trees and more secluded areas where she could be by herself. She also noticed an island in the middle of Lake Oakwood, so she knew that was the place for her because it looked more attractive than the other ones.

Penny looked around for a manager's office to the campsite. When she found the building, she went inside to talk with him about leaving her trailer in a secluded area.

"Good afternoon. My name is Bill Walters, and I'm the new manager here at Lake Oakwood Campsite."

"It's nice to meet you."

"By the way, you look familiar. Is your name Susan Mason?"

"No," Penny replied. "My name is Penny Marshall.

"Okay. You just look like someone I know except for the hair color and style. You live in Lakeview Apartments, don't you?"

Penny took a deep breath before she responded. "I'm sorry, I don't know you."

"I didn't mean to upset you."

"That's all right. I'm just leery of strangers," Penny replied.

Who is this guy? He knows me, but how could he? I don't remember him, Penny thought.

"I understand. What can I do for you?

"I'd like to leave my trailer in a secluded area so I don't have to take it with me all the time. I also like camping and having my privacy."

The manager told her that she could park anywhere she wanted to because it would be safe. She thanked the manager and walked back to her van.

After that, Penny drove around the campsite and chose a secluded area near the main entrance of the campsite. She knew this was the right place for her because oak trees surrounded the area and people wouldn't know she was there.

After she walked back to her van, she climbed inside, so she could drive back to her apartment.

On the way, she thought about the things the manager said to her. *Who is Bill Walters? I don't know anyone by that name, but he sure knows me. I wonder if he's wearing some kind of disguise so I couldn't recognize him. I thought people wouldn't recognize me since I'm wearing a wig. Abby didn't recognize me. I'll have to do something different when I get back to my apartment, but I don't know what I could do.*

Chapter Eight
The Intruder

When Penny returned to her apartment, she parked her van in the parking space in front of her building and climbed out so she could walk inside.

"Hi, Miss Marshall. How are you today?" Mr. Martin asked. "By the way, I like your hair style and color."

"Thanks. I'm doing all right. I just returned from checking out the campsites."

"Did you like them?"

"Yes. I left my trailer in a secluded area where I'm going to camp out sometime."

"That's a good idea," Mr. Martin said.

"How are you doing today?"

"I'm doing fine. So far it's been a peaceful Saturday morning, and nothing unusual has happened," Mr. Martin replied.

"I've had a peaceful morning, too. I just hope it stays that way."

"I'll agree. By the way, you look nice today. Green is a good color on you," Mr. Martin said. "Your make-up also enhances your natural beauty."

"Thank you for the compliments. You look nice in your blue suit."

"Thank you. I've got to be going, so I hope your day continues to be a peaceful one."

"So do I," Penny replied, with a smile.

Penny took the elevator to the second floor. When the elevator stopped and the doors opened, she walked in the direction of her apartment. As she approached her door, she trembled with fear because she saw her door slightly ajar. "What's going on? I'm positive I shut the door and locked it before I went to the grocery store," she said to herself.

Penny reached for the doorknob, but fear started to overwhelm her - her heart beat heavily, her hand trembled, and perspiration dripped from her face. She cautiously opened the door and saw her sofa cushions tossed on the floor, the desk drawers pulled out, papers strewn everywhere, pictures on the wall were moved as if someone was looking for a safe, and chairs turned over. "Why me? Who could have done this and why? What was the intruder looking for? Oh no! I hope it wasn't..."

Penny felt the pit of her stomach tighten as she thought of the intruder. She became tense as she wondered if he was still inside her apartment. She didn't want to confront whoever had been or might still be in her apartment, but she wanted to continue her search.

As Penny walked into the kitchen, her eyes almost popped out when she noticed that someone had opened her cupboard doors and refrigerator door. She saw cans of food, dishes, and utensils scattered on the counter tops, which left her very little space to set her grocery sacks except on the square kitchen table, which already had several items on it from the cupboards and drawers. She was glad she didn't buy anything perishable because she didn't want to touch anything in case the police wanted to check for fingerprints. All she wanted to do was to find out who had been in her apartment and why?

"What could the intruder be looking for in my kitchen? There isn't anything here except food, cookware, dishes, and silverware, so it doesn't make sense. I hope he isn't hiding somewhere."

Penny didn't want to confront him, but she wanted to check out the rest of her apartment. As she walked slowly into her bedroom, she saw her blue covers tossed on the floor, the drawers of her oak wood chest and dresser pulled out, her clothes strewn on the bed and on her light blue carpet, and her closet door open. It was obvious to her that someone had searched for something, but she didn't know what it could be.

Could it have something to do with one of my computer disks? Is there some information on it that this guy wanted? If he were looking for some information on my computer, why would he turn my whole apartment upside down just to look for something on the computer disks? It has to be something else, but what? Penny thought, as she pondered over the questions that flooded her mind.

Finally, Penny entered the bathroom and stood stiff as a board as she stared at a man's body lying in the bathtub. Oh no! It can't be him! Penny thought. Now I may have to leave again.

Without checking to see if he was dead or alive, she turned and dashed out of her apartment. She rushed down the hall to Abby's apartment and pounded on the door.

When Abby opened the door, Penny brushed passed Abby and stood in the middle of the living room breathing hard and trying to speak.

"Penny, what's wrong?"

"M.....y. M.....y. M.....y." Penny stuttered and shook like a leaf, as she pointed anxiously toward her apartment.

"Let's sit down on the sofa and talk. I'll get you something to drink to help you calm down."

Penny couldn't sit down because she was too nervous about what she saw in her apartment. Instead, she paced the floor until Abby came back into the living room. When she returned, Penny drank a few sips of water.

"What's going on," Abby said, as she talked calmly to Penny.

"The... The... The...," Penny still pointed anxiously toward her apartment.

"Penny, are you trying to tell me something about your apartment?"

"Ye... Ye..., Yes," Penny replied, still not being able to talk.

"What about your apartment?" Abby asked.

"The... there's a b... o... d...y."

"What?"

"A body."

"Where?"

"In my apartment," Penny replied, as she took a few more sips of water.

"Maybe we should call the police?" Abby suggested.

"Wait. Come.... with.... me.... first."

"Why?"

"He....might....not....be....dead," Penny replied, as she took a breath between words.

"Okay. Let's go back to your apartment first."

"Thank....you," Penny said, as she began to calm down.

Abby and Penny walked out the door headed toward Penny's apartment. When they approached her apartment, they stopped and listened. "Wait. I heard something," Abby said.

"I did, too. Let's get out of here."

As both girls turned and dashed toward Abby's apartment, they stumbled over each other. (They were not aware that someone saw them scrambling to get up and dash toward Abby's apartment.) They managed to get up and run to the door. Abby opened the door, and when both girls were inside, Abby locked the door, and then they collapsed on the sofa and tried to catch their breath.

"What's going on in your apartment?" Abby asked.

"I don't know. When I came home from the grocery store, I saw my door slightly ajar. I cautiously opened my door and was stunned when I saw everything tossed on the floor. As I continued to search my apartment, I saw everything scattered over the kitchen counters, over my bed, and floors. I need to go back there and see if the body's still there. Please come with me."

"Are you crazy? What about the noise we heard coming from your apartment? The intruder could still be there," Abby replied, as she tried to calm down.

"I know, but I've got to find out about the body."

"Don't you think we should call the police first?" Abby asked.

"No," Penny replied, abruptly.

"Why?"

"I just can't right now. I can't explain my reason."

"Do you know this guy?"

"No," Penny said. She didn't want to reveal to Abby that she thought she knew him, and she didn't want to call the police until she knew more.

"Okay."

Abby and Penny hurried back to Penny's apartment, and when they opened the bathroom door, Penny blurted out, "He's gone!"

"Are you sure a body was here?"

"Yes. He was lying in the tub."

"Where did he go?" Abby asked.

"I don't know. How can a dead body disappear?"

"It's obvious he wasn't dead. Maybe he was the one who caused the crash we heard earlier?" Abby suggested.

"If that's true, he could still be in the building because I wasn't gone that long," Penny replied, anxiously.

"Calm down."

"That's easy for you to say because it wasn't your place that was broken into," Penny snapped.

"No, and I hope it isn't, but we need to calm down."

"I'm sorry I'm upset, but I can't stay here. H ... could return," Penny said, a little calmer.

"What?"

"Nothing."

"Do you know the intruder?"

"No."

"Okay. You just acted like you knew him."

"I don't know him. I don't want to stay here because he might return, and I don't want to confront him."

"I understand. I'm not sure how I'd react if it had been my apartment. Why don't you gather up a few things and stay with me tonight," Abby suggested.

"Okay. I'll do that because I really don't want to stay here in my apartment in case he comes back."

After Penny quickly gathered up some clothes, make-up, her mystery books, journal, pens, and other personal items, they walked back to Abby's apartment. Penny took her belongings into the spare bedroom while Abby walked into the kitchen.

When Abby returned to the living room, she saw Penny sitting on the sofa. "I made some hot chocolate and brought in a few chocolate chip cookies for us while we talk about what happened," Abby said, as she set the tray on the walnut coffee table that was in front of the blue leather sofa.

After a few sips of her hot chocolate and a chocolate chip cookie, Penny started telling Abby again what she had seen when she returned from the grocery store. Abby asked Penny if she thought the intruder had taken anything. Penny told her she wasn't sure because she was too frightened to stay there and find out. Penny thought for a minute and told Abby that she didn't think the intruder took anything.

"Maybe he took something when we heard the crash," Abby suggested.

"The man in the bathtub might not have been the one we heard," Penny replied.

"That's possible, but if it wasn't him, then someone else broke into your apartment."

"Oh no. I hope not because I know what the one guy looks like, but I wouldn't have any idea about another intruder."

"I understand, and it's possible it was just the one man you saw and heard," Abby replied.

"I hope so. I need to call the police and report the break-in," Penny said, as she picked up the phone, which was on the oak lamp table beside the sofa.

The desk sergeant answered the phone, and Penny told him someone broke into her place and scattered her possessions everywhere.

"Where do you live?" Sergeant Masters asked.

"Lakeview Apartments, Apartment 201, which is across the street from Crystal Lake. I'm in the first building on the left as you come through the main entrance."

"Where are you now?"

"In apartment 215. It's my girl friend's apartment."

"What's her name?"

"Abby Fisher."

"Thanks for the information. I'll send Detective Mallory over within an hour."

Penny hung up the phone and told Abby that Detective Mallory would be there in an hour. Penny and Abby sat on the sofa and tried to figure out who the man was in the bathtub and why he was lying there pretending to be dead.

"Have you seen the man before?" Abby asked.

"No," Penny replied. She still didn't want to reveal anything to Abby.

Even though he looked familiar, he could have had on a disguise.

Suddenly she thought about Abe Salters and wondered if it could be him. *I hate him for what he did to me. He lied to me and destroyed my life. If I hadn't seen the e-mail letter about me and what he had done, I wouldn't have known he lied to me. He led me to believe I was his child, and now I'm not sure who I am or anything about my past, Penny* thought to herself.

Penny didn't want to confront Abe Salters because of what he had done several years ago. On the other hand, she couldn't understand why he would trash her apartment since she didn't have anything he'd want; unless, he wanted to make sure she was the one he was after.

"Penny, are you all right? You look like you're in a place far away."

Bringing her thoughts captive, Penny told Abby she was all right. "This whole thing has me disturbed because I don't know why he would trash my apartment."

"I don't either. It must be disturbing, but he must have known you."

"No."

Suddenly, Penny thought about the other apartment owners and wondered if he lived in the complex or a relative of an apartment owner. She hoped he didn't live nearby because she wanted him out of her life.

In a few minutes, Abby asked Penny if she had remembered anything that the intruder might have taken from her apartment, but Penny told her she hadn't thought of anything. She didn't want to lie to Abby, but the only thing she thought of were the data disks from her computers. She had two computers: a desktop and a laptop.

I don't want to face the intruder again. Maybe I can go back and grab a few things. Then, I can leave for a few days, but where do I go? Penny thought.

Abby suggested they go back to Penny's apartment to see if the intruder had taken anything. As they walked out the door, Detective Mallory, who was about 6 feet and average weight, was dressed in a brown suit, white shirt, and brown dress shoes, greeted them. "I'm Detective Mallory. Are you Miss Marshall and Miss Fisher?"

"Yes. I'm Penny Marshall, and this is Abby Fisher."

"We were headed to Penny's apartment to see if anything was missing," Abby said.

"I see. Let's go check," Detective Mallory said.

They entered the apartment and saw that everything was still out of place. "Is this the way you found it?" Detective Mallory asked.

"Yes," Penny replied.

"I want to see the rest of the place, but please don't touch anything. I want the crime-scene officers to come and check things out."

They continued to search the other rooms, and Detective Mallory concluded that somebody had to be searching for something in particular, but he couldn't imagine what it could be. He also told Penny and Abby that he couldn't understand why they would search the kitchen and remove the contents from the cupboards and drawers, or leave the refrigerator door open.

Abby told Detective Mallory that he might have done it to throw everyone off track. Detective Mallory thought she might be right.

After they searched the apartment, they walked into the hall.

"Let's go back to your apartment Miss Fisher and finish our discussion. I also want to call the crime-scene officers and have them dust for prints."

They entered Abby's apartment, and Abby showed Detective Mallory where the phone was. He sat on the sofa and called the crime-scene officers. After that, he began his investigation.

Chapter Nine

The Investigation

Before Detective Mallory started asking his questions, Abby asked, "Could I get you something to drink?"

"Coffee would be fine if it's not too much trouble."

"No trouble at all. I just made some fresh coffee this morning."

"Okay."

"Penny, would you like something to drink?"

"Hot chocolate if you have some."

"Sure."

Abby got out a tray, three coffee mugs, napkins, dainty cookies, cream pitcher, and some sugar packets. She poured the coffee in two of the mugs and fixed hot chocolate in the other mug for Penny, and then she took the tray into the living room and set it on the coffee table in front of the sofa.

Detective Mallory picked up his cup and took a sip. "Good coffee."

"Thanks."

"Penny, can you describe the intruder?" Detective Mallory asked.

"I'll try. I just glanced at him and took off. He was average weight and height, had short black hair, and had on blue slacks and a blue plaid shirt. That's all I know," Penny said.

"That's fine. I can understand how frightened you must have been when you saw him."

"I was. I just wanted to escape."

When they heard a knock on the door, Abby got up to answer it. The crime-scene officers walked into the room. Detective Mallory stood up and asked them what they found out. They told him they found three sets of fingerprints that belonged to Penny, Abby, and a man. They told Detective Mallory they were going to the station and see if they could find out the identity of the man's fingerprints. He thanked them, and then he sat down and began to question Penny and Abby about the intruder. He asked Abby if she had seen the intruder. She told him that she hadn't because Penny came to get her after she had seen him, and when they returned to Penny's apartment, the man disappeared.

Detective Mallory asked Penny if she thought it was possible the intruder had seen her when she entered the bathroom. She told him she didn't think it was possible because his eyes were closed.

Detective Mallory told them that it was a good thing he didn't see her because she might still be in danger. "Where are you going to stay tonight?" Detective Mallory asked.

"With Abby because I don't want to stay in my apartment, but I need to grab a few things."

"I'll have a security guard nearby throughout the night in case the intruder returns."

"Thanks," Penny replied.

"I'm also going to interview the other tenants to see if they noticed anything unusual."

"Is it all right if Abby and I go back and search the apartment to see if anything was taken?"

"Sure. You can do that while I continue my investigation. I want to interview the other tenants.

As Detective Mallory stood up to leave, the phone rang. Abby answered the phone and said it was one of the crime-scene officers. Detective Mallory took the phone and wrote down the information when he hung up he said, "They have the identity of the man."

"Who is it?" Penny asked.

"Abe Salters."

Penny looked stunned for a few minutes.

"Penny, are you all right?" Abby asked.

"Yes."

"Do you know the man?" Detective Mallory asked.

"I'm not sure." Penny didn't want to reveal anything at the time because she didn't think the man looked like Abe Salters because of his hair. Then, she realized he could have changed the color of his hair and style.

"Okay. I'm going to continue my investigation, and I'll get back with you soon."

He walked toward the door and then turned around. He told them he would like to get together in a couple of hours to discuss their findings.

Penny and Abby walked down the hall to Penny's apartment. Penny felt fear swell up inside as she cautiously entered her apartment. She didn't want the intruder to return. They looked around the living room and saw that everything was the same as they left it.

Penny and Abby started cleaning up the living room. Penny gathered up her papers that were on the floor and put them in her backpack. Then, she picked up the case for her laptop and disks and another bag for her electric cord, batteries, and other accessories.

After Penny put her desk drawers where they belonged, she took out a small zipper bag and gathered up some pens, white outs, hi-lighters, pencils, erasers, markers, colored pencils, package of staples, and her stapler. Then, she put everything in the bag and placed the zipper bag in her backpack.

Abby picked up the cushions and put the chairs where they belonged. Then, she hung the pictures like they should be and organized the rest of the room.

When the living room was clean, they cleaned up the kitchen and bedroom. As they looked through the apartment, Abby asked Penny if she noticed anything missing. Penny told her that she hadn't found anything missing so far.

After Penny gathered up the things she wanted to take with her, she locked the door, and they walked to Abby's apartment.

In the meantime, Detective Mallory walked downstairs to the manager's office. He knocked on the door and waited. "Mr. Martin. I'm Detective Mallory."

"It's nice to meet you. How can I help you?"

"I'm investigating the burglary that occurred this morning," Detective Mallory said.

"Burglary! Where?" Mr. Martin asked. "Please come in."

Detective Mallory entered the apartment and sat on the brown sofa. He started writing down the information about the case.

"It was in Miss Marshall's apartment."

"What!" Mr. Martin said, with a surprised look on his face. "Is she all right?"

"Yes. She's shook up, but she'll be all right. Did you see anyone lurking around here this morning?" Detective Mallory asked.

"Not really. Wait a minute. I do remember a man asking me about someone named Susan Salters and where her apartment number.

"What time did you talk to the person?" Detective Mallory asked.

"Around 9:00 this morning. I told him I didn't have anyone registered here by that name."

"He showed me a picture of Susan Salters. I looked at the picture and realized that it was Penny Marshall, but I don't know why he called her Susan Salters. He told me he wanted to surprise her because he said he was a friend of hers when she lived in California."

"I see. Do you know his name, or what he looked like?" Detective Mallory asked.

Mr. Martin gave him the description of the man he saw. It was the exact description of the man lying in Penny's bathtub.

"Thanks. He's the one Penny found lying in her bathtub."

"What! Is he dead?"

"No. He seems to have disappeared," Detective Mallory replied.

"Oh no! I saw him was this morning before Penny returned from the grocery store. He's registered in Apartment 200."

"Okay. Thanks for your help."

"I'll let you know if I see him again," Mr. Martin said.

"Thanks."

Detective Mallory walked back up to the second floor. When he opened the door to the stairway, he saw Penny and Abby in the hall. "Miss Marshall, Miss Fisher did you notice anything missing?"

"No. We cleaned up the apartment since the crime-scene officers were finished."

"That's fine."

"Did you find out anything?" Penny asked.

"I noticed a few things missing. Shall we go inside and discuss it?"

"Sure," Abby replied, as she unlocked the door.

They entered the living room and sat down. "I just left Mr. Martin's apartment, and he told me that a man, fitting the description you gave me, asked about someone named Susan Salters this morning. He showed Mr. Martin a picture of the girl, and Mr. Martin told me it was a picture of you. He also told me the guy was a friend of yours from California. Can you tell me what's going on here?"

"No," Penny replied. She didn't want to admit the truth, yet.

"Is your name Susan Salters?"

"No. I'm Penny Marshall." *Penny couldn't believe his question. What's going on here? He's the second person who asked me if I was Susan Salters. Why is this happening to me? How did they find out I was living in Lakeview?*

"Okay. I still need to investigate the other tenants on this floor."

"That's fine. We'll be here," Detective Mallory said.

"I'll return within an hour and let you know what I found out," Abby said.

Detective Mallory left so he could talk to the other tenants. He knocked on the apartment next to Penny's apartment, and a young woman around 20 years old came to the door.

"I'm Detective Mallory, and I'm investigating a crime that occurred on this floor early this morning. May I come in?"

"Yes. Please sit down," the woman said, as she pointed to the green sofa. "My name is Callie Green.

Detective Mallory sat down, and Callie sat across from him.

"Did you hear anything shortly after 9:00 this morning?"

"No, I'm sorry I didn't hear anything."

"Did you see anyone lurking around the hall who didn't live here?"

"I saw a man with brown hair in the hall this morning who was acting kind of strange."

"Strange. What do you mean?"

"I noticed that he was standing around in the hall for awhile, and then he disappeared. I'm not sure of the time. I just moved here last week and usually stay in my apartment, so I haven't met anyone except Abby and Penny."

"If you see anything unusual, please call me. Here's my card." Detective Mallory pulled out his card and handed it to her.

"Okay, I will."

Detective Mallory left and walked to another neighbor. He knocked on the door, but nobody answered so he walked down the hall to another apartment. This time a woman, who was about 30 years old, answered the door.

"I'm Detective Mallory, and I'm investigating a burglary that occurred this morning."

"My name is Karen Brady. Please come in."

Detective Mallory entered the apartment and glanced around. Then, he sat on the sofa. "Have you seen anyone lurking around the halls this morning?"

"No. However, a middle-aged couple in the apartment across the hall just moved in last Tuesday. It's strange, though."

"What do you mean?"

"They didn't have much furniture, and I haven't seen them together. They stay in their apartment most of the time."

"Okay. Maybe I'll talk to them, too."

Detective Mallory walked across the hall to talk to the couple. He knocked on the door, and a middle-aged woman opened the door.

"May I help you?"

"I'm Detective Mallory. I'm investigating an incident that occurred this morning. May I come in?"

"No. I don't know anything about any burglary, and I'm busy."

"What about your husband?" Detective Mallory asked, as he glanced around the room. He wasn't able to see much since the woman blocked his view. He also glanced at her, and noticed that something was unusual about her, but he wasn't sure.

"He doesn't know anything either."

"May I talk to him?"

"He's not here. I'm busy and need to get back to work."

"Okay. Here's my card. If you think of anything, please call me. By the way, what's your name?"

"Why do you ask?"

"I need it for my records."

"Annie Salyers," the woman snapped, as shut the door before Detective Mallory could say anything else. *Something is mysterious about her.* Detective Mallory thought to himself on the way back to Abby's apartment.

After that, he returned to Abby's apartment. He knocked on the door, and Abby opened it. He walked inside and sat on the sofa.

"Did you find out anything?" Abby asked.

"Yes. One of the tenants told me he noticed a man with brown hair. Didn't you say he had black hair?"

"Yes."

"That's strange. I don't understand how two guys with similar descriptions can have different hair color," Detective Mallory said.

"Maybe there are two guys," Abby suggested.

"You mean twins," Detective Mallory replied.

"Maybe," Abby said.

"That's possible. It would explain the different hair color descriptions."

"Do you know any twins?" Detective Mallory asked Penny.

"No. I don't."

"Maybe the guy used a disguise so that someone wouldn't recognize him," Abby suggested.

"That could be," Detective Mallory replied.

"There's also something else."

"What?" Abby asked.

"Another tenant acted really strange. A middle-aged woman came to the door, and when I asked her to come in, she refused to let me inside. She said she was busy. She was also rude when I told her that I was investigating a case and the possibility of seeing anyone lurking around the hallway. Wait a minute. This is strange."

"What?" Abby asked.

"She mentioned burglary, and I didn't say anything about a burglary."

"That is strange, so she has to be hiding something," Abby said.

"That's not all. She didn't want to give me her name, but she finally told me she was Annie Salyers."

"I'm doing a writing assignment for a woman named Annie Salyers," Abby replied.

"Then you've met her," Detective Mallory said.

"Yes. Only for a short time. She dropped off her manuscripts she wanted Penny and me to proofread and edit for her."

"I see," Detective Mallory said. "Another neighbor told me the middle-aged woman and her husband were never seen together. It made me wonder what was going on or if she was a woman. Penny, do you know someone named Annie Salyers?"

"No," Penny replied.

"You mean you think she could be disguised as a man?" Abby asked.

"That's just a theory."

"This is getting complicated," Penny commented.

"I know. I'm not sure what to think about this situation," Detective Mallory said.

"We still don't know who entered my apartment and why," Penny said.

"I know. I'm going to talk to Mr. Martin about the couple in Apartment 200."

"Apartment 200!" Penny exclaimed. "That's across the hall from my apartment."

"I know. Mr. Martin said that a man named Abe Salters was registered in Apartment 200. Since he seems to know you, I'll post a guard in the building so we can keep an eye on him."

"Thanks," Penny replied.

"I'd like for you to come to the station and look at some mug shots."

"That's fine. When?" Penny asked.

"Are you free now?"

"Yes. Can Abby come with me?"

"Sure," Detective Mallory replied, as he opened the door to leave."

Penny and Abby picked up their sweaters and walked into the hall. Abby locked her door, and they walked downstairs to Abby's car.

When they arrived at the station, Detective Mallory led them to a private room. Penny started looking through the mug shots. Half way through the book, Penny spotted a photo she thought might be the guy she saw. She told Detective Mallory about the picture. She told him he looked like the intruder except for the hair color and a small mole on the side of his face.

"This case has become more complicated because I have a description of three guys with similar features except for minor differences," Detective Mallory said.

"I agree," Abby replied.

"Thanks for coming and looking at the photos. We're going to continue our investigation until we locate the intruder."

"We want to help anyway we can," Abby replied.

"I'll be in touch with you later," Detective Mallory said.

"By the way, I'm glad I can work with you on a case. Since I'm a freelance writer and an amateur detective, I want to spend time searching for clues and other types of research. It helps my writing improve," Abby said.

"No problem. I can always use extra help," Detective Mallory replied with a smile.

"I'm also a freelance writer and amateur detective," Penny said.

"That's good. A security guard will be here soon. His name is Officer Watkins, and he's about my height and weight. He'll be dressed in plain clothes so he doesn't stand out, and he's also going to stay in one of the vacant apartments on your floor."

"Thanks," Penny replied.

"I hope nothing else happens," Abby said.

"I do, too. I'm curious about the middle-aged woman who seemed so mysterious. Something didn't add up with her, so I'm going to keep an eye on that apartment."

"Sounds good. We'll let you know if we see anything, too," Abby replied.

"Also, let me know if you remember anything else."

"I will," Penny said.

When they arrived at Abby's apartment, Abby told Penny she had some chicken tenders, roasted potatoes, Cole Slaw, and fruit punch for supper.

Penny told Abby that was all right with her.

They walked into the kitchen, and Abby took out the chicken tenders and potatoes and put them in pans and then in the oven.

After that, they set the table, and then Abby took the food out of the oven, placed them on plates, and set them on the table. Penny took out the Cole Slaw, and Abby poured the fruit punch into their glasses.

"I was thinking about the three guys. Which one do you believe was in your apartment?" Abby asked, as they started eating their supper.

"I don't know because I really didn't get a good look at him," Penny said.

"Do you have any idea why he was in your apartment?"

"No," Penny replied.

"Maybe when the police find him, you'll know who he was and why he was there."

"Maybe. I'm trying not to think about it," Penny said.

"That's fine. We can talk about other things."

"Thanks."

"You can sleep in the guest room tonight. Did you bring some clothes?"

"Yes."

"After supper, let's work on our writing assignments," Abby suggested.

"That's a good idea."

Penny and Abby did the dishes and cleaned up the kitchen.

After that, they took out their writing supplies and started working. They finished their assignments that were due on Wednesday, and then they started reading their books for the book reviews that were due Friday. They weren't very long, so both of them knew they would be able to finish reading the books quickly and write the reviews.

About 10:00, they started getting drowsy and decided to get ready for bed. Penny walked into the spare bedroom, picked up her laptop, and wrote in her hidden journal. She didn't want anyone to locate the private information about her past, and her life in California.

Crimewriter's Journal

I thought I was free from my past when I left California, but now it's caught up with me. What am I going to do? I don't want Abby to get hurt because of me. Maybe I should disappear for a while. Who is this Annie Salyers? Oh no - Maybe she's Annie Salters. If she is Annie Salters, then they're both here. Why can't they leave me alone? Why did Detective Mallory think she might be a man? Did Abe disguise himself as Annie, or did she just act like a man to throw Detective Mallory off? I don't want them to find me, so I need to get away for a few days. I know. Nobody would think to look there. At least I hope they wouldn't. I need to disguise myself again so nobody will recognize me.

Chapter Ten
Penny's Disappearance

Penny arose early in the morning so she could take a shower and wash her hair before she started her day even though she wasn't sure what she planned on doing, but she was happy that Abby had her stay with her last night because she didn't want to sleep in her own apartment after the break-in. After her shower, she donned her blue slacks, white blouse, blue sweater that matched her slacks, white socks, and navy blue leather slip-ons, and then she walked into the living room and noticed Abby sitting on the sofa and drinking some orange juice.

"Would you like some orange juice or something to eat now?"

"Not yet because I need to get something from my apartment."

"Are you sure you want to go to your apartment after what happened last night?"

"I'll be all right."

"Okay. I'm going to take a shower and then get breakfast, so it will be ready when you return."

Penny opened the door and looked around to see if anyone was nearby, but since she didn't notice anyone, she walked cautiously down the hall to her apartment and unlocked her door. She quickly entered her apartment, shut the door behind her, and locked it because she didn't want to confront any more intruders while she was inside her apartment. When she approached her desk, her eyes almost popped out because she noticed the following note:

Beware because I'm watching you, and you
won't know when I'll appear, and you won't
recognize me. I know you aren't staying in
your apartment, but I will find you, so watch
out! Whoever is protecting you will be harmed,
too, unless you escape, but will you be safe then?

As Penny read the note, her heart pounded and her body trembled with fear because she was afraid for her life and especially for Abby. Thoughts flooded her mind as she pondered over her circumstances. *Who could have written the note? Could it have been the intruder, and if so when? Why would the intruder want to harm Abby?*

Penny was so confused about the break-in and wondered if the intruder was Abe Salters. Now that she received this note, her situation became more difficult and confusing. "Was the intruder watching me? If he was, then he must know I'm staying with Abby," Penny said to herself. She realized now what she had to do, and that was to leave Abby's apartment at least for a few days so someone wouldn't harm Abby.

While Penny started to grab a few of her things, her heart pounded faster because she thought she heard a noise somewhere inside her apartment. Not wanting to confront the intruder, she quickly picked up what she needed and dashed out the door. Without realizing it, she dropped the note on a stack of papers that were on the floor, and then she ran down the hall to Abby's apartment.

As Penny rushed inside, she realized Abby was still in the shower, so she dashed into her room, grabbed her suitcase and put her clothes and personal items inside, and then she grabbed her backpack so she could put her other items inside. After that, she picked up her laptop and slipped out quietly because she wanted to leave without alarming Abby. Penny didn't want Abby to know about the note and why she had to leave in a hurry.

Penny hurried outside to her van, quickly unlocked it, loaded it, climbed inside, and headed north. As she drove north to the campsite where she decided to camp for a few days, she thought about God and wondered why he had allowed this to happen to her because she thought things were beginning to work out for her in Lakeview, and now she wasn't sure what was going on. She couldn't understand how someone from California figured out her destination, which was Lakeview. Now, in addition to worrying about herself, she worried about Abby because she didn't want anyone to harm her.

Meanwhile, back at Abby's apartment, Abby came out of the bathroom and didn't see Penny, so she assumed she was still in her apartment. As Abby walked into the kitchen to fix breakfast, she thought about Detective Mallory and expected to hear from him today about his investigation. She hoped that he had some more information about the intruder so that Penny could relax and not worry about her circumstances.

When Detective Mallory arrived at Lakeview Apartments, he parked his blue and white sedan in the visitor's parking space, and as he walked inside, Mr. Martin, who was dressed in his brown suit and brown tie, greeted him at the entrance. "Hello Detective Mallory. How are you this morning?"

"I'm fine, and how about yourself?"

"I'm fine, too. I'm thankful that it's been peaceful around here this morning since all the commotion we had here yesterday. By the way, have you found out anything?"

"As a matter of fact, I have found out a few things, but it's beginning to be a little complicated because we have descriptions of three men who are alike in physical stature, but they have a few minor characteristics that are different."

"I can understand how that could be a little complicated, but I'm positive you'll find a solution soon," Mr. Martin commented.

"Yes, it does, and we're trying to sort through the evidence we have," Detective Mallory replied.

"If I can help you in any way, please let me know."

"Thanks for the offer. I'm sure I'll be visiting with you again about the tenants or something I might find out, but I hope it's not another investigation involving another crime.

"I'll agree, especially something else that involves Miss Marshall and Miss Fisher because they've been through enough."

"That's true. I'm on my way up to see them right now, so I'll talk to you later."

Detective Mallory walked up the stairs to Abby's apartment so he could visit with Penny, and when he arrived at Abby's apartment, he knocked on the door and waited for Abby or Penny to come and open the door.

After waiting a few minutes, he was about to knock again, but Abby opened the door and greeted him. "Detective Mallory. Please come in. I'm sorry it took me a little while to answer the door, but I was getting ready to fix breakfast for Penny and me."

"That's okay. I know it's early, but I wanted to visit with Miss Marshall this morning. By the way, how are you this morning?"

"I'm doing okay considering the break-in at Penny's apartment, and how nerve racking it was for both of us."

"I understand how you two must feel because it was a scary situation since Penny's privacy was invaded, and now she had to move in with you for awhile."

"That's true. Penny went to her apartment this morning to pick up something that she needed, but she must have returned by now and is probably in her room, so I'll get her."

Abby walked to Penny's room and knocked on the door, but when she didn't hear anything, she opened the door and looked around. She realized Penny wasn't in her room or the bathroom, so she looked in her closet and noticed that her clothes were missing.

Rushing into the living room, Abby announced rather quickly that she couldn't locate Penny and that her clothes were gone.

"Penny's not in her room or the bathroom, and her clothes are gone. What could have happened to her? She told me she was going to her apartment, pick up something, and would return shortly, so why are her clothes missing?"

"Maybe she decided to return to her apartment instead of staying here," Detective Mallory suggested, calmly.

"I don't see how that's possible because she told me she was going to pick up something and would be back. I told her that was okay, and I would have breakfast ready when she returned, but that was about an hour ago. I had taken a shower and donned my clothes, and when I came out of the bathroom, I didn't see her, so I thought she was still in her apartment. I didn't think she'd wanted to stay in her apartment for any length of time because she was too frightened last night after the break-in. That's why I suggested to her that she sleep in my guest bedroom. She was here last night, but she wasn't here this morning. Now, I'm worried about her."

"We need to return to her apartment just to make sure that she didn't return there," Detective Mallory suggested.

"That's a good idea. I just hope the intruder didn't harm her."

"I'm sure she'll be all right," Detective Mallory replied, with assurance.

They walked down the hall to Penny's apartment, but they couldn't locate her, so Detective Mallory and Abby didn't know what to think about Penny's disappearance or what happened to her clothes.

Abby wondered if Penny had returned to gather up her clothes and other personal items when she was in the bathroom, or if someone else had entered her apartment and nabbed Penny and her belongings.

"Where could she be? It's not like her to disappear like this. She would have told me if she was going to leave," Abby said.

"It does seem weird for her to leave after her place was broken into, unless..."

"Unless what?"

"Unless...Well, I hate to think about it or even mention it to you because of what's happened and how you seem to be close to Penny, but the only solution I can think of was that the intruder came back and kidnapped her?" Detective Mallory replied.

"I hope that didn't happen," Abby said, with a worried expression on her face.

"I didn't want to upset you, but I'm trying to think of the possibilities."

"I understand. Wait a minute - I don't see how that can be possible because her clothes are gone, too, so if she was kidnapped, why would the person collect her clothes and other personal items Penny had in here?"

"I see what you're saying, and I also wondered when they could have done that if you were in the bathroom and then in the kitchen because you would have heard something since your apartment isn't that big," Detective Mallory replied.

"Maybe we need to talk to the neighbors just in case someone might have seen her this morning or heard something or searched her apartment for some clues," Abby suggested.

"That's a good idea because it's possible someone could have heard something, and maybe we could uncover some clues as to her whereabouts, so you can search Penny's apartment while I talk with the neighbors again," Detective Mallory said.

"What kind of clues are you thinking about?" Abby asked.

"I'm not sure, but you mentioned that you're both freelance writers, so maybe Penny stored some information on her computer that would help us?" Detective Mallory suggested.

"It's possible Penny has some pertinent information on her desktop computer or her laptop. Wait - Her laptop is gone because I didn't see it in her room."

"Something is going on here, so I need to check with the neighbor who seemed a little strange yesterday, and see how they react today or if they have noticed anything this morning."

"I'll check Penny's apartment to see what clues I can find on her computer."

Detective Mallory walked next door to Apartment 200 and knocked a couple of times before a middle-aged man opened the door. "What can I do for you again?"

"My name is Detective Mallory, and I'd like to ask you a few questions."

"I answered your questions yesterday."

"Okay," Detective Mallory said, a little puzzled.

"By the way, what's your name?"

"Why do you need to know that?" the man replied, as he flexed his fingers a few times.

"I need it for my records," Detective Mallory replied, as he opened up his notebook to write down the information.

"Abe Salters."

"Thanks," Detective Mallory said, as he wrote the name in his pad. After that, he showed the man a picture of Penny and asked him if he had ever seen the woman.

"Not this morning, why?"

"She's disappeared, and her friend, Abby, and I are trying to locate her."

"When did this woman disappear?"

"Sometime this morning," Detective Mallory replied. "She went to her apartment to pick up something, and she wasn't seen after that.

"Good."

"What?"

"Nothing. Is that all because I'm busy right now and something has just come up," Abe Salters asked, as he flexed his fingers and blinked his eyes nervously.

"Okay. Thanks for your help, but I'll probably be talking to you again, so don't leave town," Detective Mallory said, as he turned to walk down the hall to Abby's apartment.

Detective Mallory knocked on the door, and just as Abby opened the door, he saw the neighbor, Abe Salters, open his door and enter the hallway. Detective Mallory quickly entered Abby's apartment and shut the door slightly, so he could watch Abe Salters. When he saw him go down the stairs, he told Abby to stay inside her apartment, lock the door, and not let anyone inside until he returned.

He rushed downstairs just in time to see Abe Salters leave the building and get into his car.

A few minutes later, Detective Mallory returned to Abby's apartment and knocked on the door. "It's me, Detective Mallory."

"What's going on?" Abby asked, as she unlocked the door and opened it.

"That was the neighbor in Apartment 200." Detective Mallory replied. "He just left in a hurry after I questioned him, and I thought that was a little strange because he seemed really nervous when I questioned him and told him Penny disappeared."

"Maybe he had to do something," Abby suggested.

"He acted too nervous about the questions I asked, so I think he's hiding something or someone."

"What did he do?"

"He flexed his fingers several times and blinked his eyes nervously during our conversation, especially when I questioned him about Penny's disappearance. He also seemed happy when I said Penny disappeared, and that's when he told me something had just come up, and now, he left the building."

"Why do you think he was happy about Penny disappearing?" Abby asked.

"I'm not sure, but when I told him Penny had disappeared, he said, 'Good,' and that's not a normal response. People show more concern when they find out that someone is missing unless they were hiding something about the person."

"That's true," Abby agreed. "Could he be the intruder?"

"That's possible because he seemed too nervous when I talked to him."

"What are we going to do now?" Abby asked.

"I'm not sure. Did you find anything in Penny's apartment?"

"Not too much," Abby replied. "Last night, she had her laptop, batteries, electric cord, disks, paper, pens, and pencils with her. Now her cooler and the picnic basket are missing, and I also noticed that some more of her clothes were gone."

"I see," Detective Mallory replied. "Something else doesn't make sense about the conversation I had with Abe Salters. When I told him who I was and that I had some questions to ask him, he told me that he answered my questions yesterday."

"Wow! That is strange because I thought you talked to a woman yesterday," Abby replied.

"I did, so the only solution I can come up with is that he must be using disguises, and if he is, then this will complicate things because we won't be able to recognize him."

"What did you say?"

"Nothing because I didn't want him to know that I noticed what he said, and after I showed him Penny's picture, he told me he hadn't seen her this morning which shows me he had seen her before."

"I agree, but could he have just seen her in the hall one day as a casual meeting?"

"That's possible, but like I said earlier, he seemed really nervous when I told him Penny disappeared, and then he left in a hurry."

"Do you think he was the intruder?"

"I don't know, but there's something else," Detective Mallory said, with a curious expression on his face. "The woman said her name was Annie Salyers, and this man told me his name was Abe Salters."

"If they're married, then why are they using two different names?"

"Let's add these names to the list of clues we have."

They sat at the kitchen table and looked at the names: Annie Salyers, Abe Salters. "Look at the last name. If you change the y to t, you have Salters."

"You're right," Detective Mallory agreed. "This could be the same person, or it could be a man and wife using two different names to throw us off the track."

"He could be using a woman's disguise and a man's disguise, so I'm going to call the station and have someone do a search on the two names and see if they have a record," Detective Mallory said, as he picked up the phone to call the station. After Sergeant Masters answered the phone, Detective Mallory asked him to do a search for Annie Salyers and Abe Salters, and then he hung up.

"Where could Penny be?" Abby asked, with tears in her eyes. *God has to protect her because I can't lose Penny just after we met*, Abby thought to herself.

"I don't know, Miss Fisher, but I'm sure we'll find some more clues soon, or maybe she'll even return soon."

"Why would she take her laptop and supplies as well as the picnic basket and cooler?" Abby asked.

"Maybe she decided to run off somewhere and needed those things."

"That's possible, but why would Penny run off without saying anything to me about leaving?"

"It does seem strange for her to leave without talking to you, unless... "

"Unless what?" Abby asked curiously.

"Unless she was hiding something about her past, something frightened her, or a body wasn't in the bathtub."

"Do you think Penny could be hiding something or something frightened her?"

"It's possible," Detective Mallory replied.

"What could it be?"

"I don't know if she's hiding something or if someone or something frightened her, but I've wondered if Penny made this whole thing up." Detective Mallory questioned.

"She was so shook up when she came to my apartment that all she did was stutter, so I doubt if she if this is some kind of fantasy."

"Have you noticed anything unusual in the way Penny has been acting?"

"Not really, but I haven't paid that much attention to anything unusual because she seemed normal to me."

"How long have you known Penny?" Detective Mallory asked.

"Just a week because she just moved in here last Monday, and when we first met, we didn't get along. I bumped into her car because she stopped in the middle of the street. I thought she was going to turn into the shopping center, but she didn't, and I even paid for her car to be fixed as well as mine."

"I see."

"After that, she didn't want to talk, and she wasn't very friendly towards me when we bumped into each other in stores."

"That's interesting, so how did you two become friends?"

"Penny and I were e-mail friends, but since we used different names, we didn't know each other's real names. Penny was Crimewriter, and I was Crimesolver. When I saw her move into the apartment, I wanted to become friends and to let her know I was sorry about the accident, but she still wasn't friendly until she found out I was Crimesolver.

"How did she find out you were Crimesolver?"

"I wrote to her about the accident I had with someone."

"It's interesting how people meet," Detective Mallory commented.

"That's true. After Penny found out I was Crimesolver, we became friends and decided to start our own freelance writing service and a mystery reader's book club."

"That's good you're friends," Detective Mallory said.

"I agree. I believe God brought us together so we could become friends, work on writing, have a mystery reader's book club, and solve mysteries as amateur detectives. Neither one of us developed many friendships, so when we started writing, we just seemed to hit it off because we found out we had things in common."

"Do you know much about her past?"

"Not very much, but I do know that she doesn't have any brothers or sisters, and her parents live in California. She came to Kansas to work as a freelance writer and to be on her own. That's about all I know, but I guess that's not a lot, is it?"

"Not too much, but it does give me something to go on. Do you know where she lived in California?" Detective Mallory asked.

"No because she didn't want to talk about her past."

"Do you know if she's kept in contact with her parents or anyone in California?" Detective Mallory asked.

"She hasn't mentioned her parents or anyone in California which makes me believe she's running away from something that happened or from someone."

"Maybe they didn't have a close relationship," Detective Mallory suggested.

"That's possible, but most people will talk about their family or close friendships," Abby said.

"I agree, and that's why I wondered if there was anyone in particular she talked about?"

"Not really, but I did see her with Bob Wilson at *South of the Border*, the Mexican restaurant."

"I'm familiar with the place. It's a good place to eat. How was she then?"

"Not very friendly towards me, but she seemed to enjoy her time with Bob. However, I'm not sure how they met."

"Let's check Penny's apartment again to see if we can find anything else," Detective Mallory suggested.

"That's a good idea because I could have missed something."

"It's possible since clues are sometimes in plain sight and are overlooked easily."

Detective Mallory and Abby walked down the hall to Penny's apartment and saw Bob standing at the door.

"Abby. Hi. I've been trying to contact Penny. Do you know where she is?"

"No. She's disappeared. That's why Detective Mallory is here with me. Someone broke into her place."

"Is there anything I can do to help?"

"We're trying to come up with some clues that will help us locate Penny," Detective Mallory said.

"I'd like to help, too. I've been interested in working as an amateur detective."

"Great," Detective Mallory said.

"Abby didn't you say that Penny has a desktop computer and a laptop?"

"Yes."

"Why don't you check her computer and see if you can locate any clues on it."

"Okay."

"While you're doing that, I'll look in here and the other rooms," Detective Mallory said. "Bob, if you want to help, you can help look in here to see if we can find any clues that will help us locate Penny."

"Sure."

Abby turned on Penny's computer to search through her folders and e-mail to see if she could find any clues, but she stopped when she heard Detective Mallory blurt out. "Abby! Come here quick!" Detective Mallory hollered.

Abby dashed out of the room. "What's wrong?"

Detective Mallory handed Abby a note that he found on top of a stack of papers lying on the floor.

Abby read the note. "Oh no! Penny disappeared because someone threatened her life and mine."

"We don't know that for sure because she might not have seen the note, but it is true that someone has threatened her and you."

"Who?" Abby asked.

"I don't know, but we have to find out what's going on and where Penny is."

"I wish she had told me about the note."

"Like I just mentioned, she might not have seen the note, so she could have disappeared for another reason."

"What?" Abby asked.

"I'm not sure, but let's continue searching for more clues."

After searching for an hour, they left Penny's apartment and walked back to Abby's apartment. When they entered her apartment, Detective Mallory sat on the sofa, and Abby sat in her recliner across from him.

"I think I'll go back to the station and see if Penny has a criminal record or where she's from in California. I'll be in touch with you later."

"Okay."

"Abby, I'll return tomorrow, too, so I can help search for her," Bob said.

After Detective Mallory and Bob left, Abby took out her taco casserole and a can of pop and walked into the living room to eat. As she sat on the sofa to eat, she picked up her journal and wrote down the questions that flooded her mind.

Crimesolver's Journal

Where's Penny, and why did she disappear? This whole thing doesn't make sense because she first said there was a body, and then after we entered her bathroom, there wasn't one. Where did he go? I want to help solve this case, so I'm going to use the techniques Penny and I discussed in our book club. Since I'm an amateur detective, t know I can locate Penny.

Whoever wrote that note frightened her so much that she had to disappear, but why would someone want to harm Penny or me? Who's doing this, and why is she hiding something about her past? Did she commit a crime or was she a witness to some crime that was committed in California? Was the intruder someone from her past?

"Wait a minute!" Abby blurted out, as she stopped writing in her journal. "Could Penny be the one I'm trying to locate for her parents? Could Abe Salters have kidnapped her? If that's the case, I know why Penny was so scared."

Crimesolver continued to write in her journal. *Why didn't she talk to me more about her past? Maybe I could have helped her. Why were there three different descriptions of men instead of one? I've got to find out what happened to Penny, so I need to start searching for clues. I don't understand why did God brought us together and then allowed this to happen?*

Abby put her journal on her bedside table and then walked into the kitchen. After she opened her refrigerator, she took out the ham salad mix and fixed a ham salad sandwich, potato chips, and grabbed a can of pop out of the refrigerator. As she ate at the kitchen table, she tried to focus on her next steps to locate Penny. Since she was an amateur detective, she wanted to solve this case.

After Abby ate her lunch, she washed her dishes and cleaned up her apartment. When she was finished, she heard a knock on the door.

"Bob, hi. Please come in. Detective Mallory should be here shortly."

Just as Abby was about to shut the door, Detective Mallory approached the door and walked into Abby's apartment. He sat on the sofa. "Good morning, Bob, Abby. Have either of you heard anything from Penny?"

"Not yet."

"I checked her record, and she doesn't have a criminal record."

"I'm glad about that," Abby replied.

"However, there's something strange about her," Detective Mallory remarked.

"What?" Abby asked.

"She existed in the beginning when she was born, but she didn't seem to exist after the age of two until now," Detective Mallory replied.

"I don't understand," Abby said, with a confused expression on her face.

"There aren't any school records or any other records for a Penny Marshall."

"That's weird. What could have happened?" Suddenly, Abby's thoughts flooded her mind. *The case I'm working on has to be* Penny.

I've got to continue my investigation and see what clues I can locate.
Penny has to be the missing person.

"Abby, are you okay because you seem like you're far away?"
Detective Mallory asked.

"I'm okay," Abby replied, as she tried to focus on their
conversation.

"I know this is upsetting to you, but I'm sure we'll find her
soon," Detective Mallory replied.

"I hope so, but there is something I need to tell you."

"What?" Detective Mallory asked.

"I think Penny was kidnapped when she was two-years-old,"
Abby said.

"Kidnapped! All this time?" Bob exclaimed, with a startled
expression on his face.

"Yes. I have a case I'm working on about a girl who
disappeared when she was two-years-old, and that could explain why
you couldn't find any information on Penny during that time," Abby
replied.

"You could be right because sometimes kidnappers change
the name of their victims so people can't discover their location or find
out anything about them," Detective Mallory replied.

"That's true, and that's what I think happened to Penny," Abby
suggested.

"Do you know her real name?" Bob asked, curiously.

"From the information I've found so far, her name is Penny
Marshall. Now, I need to see if there's any information about a
kidnapping in California twenty years ago."

"Sounds good," Detective Mallory replied.

"I'll let you know when I find out something," Abby replied.

"Now, let's talk about the body. You mentioned earlier that you didn't see the body, right?" Detective Mallory asked.

"Yes."

"Then you don't know for sure if there was a body?" Bob asked.

"No. I guess not, but someone had to be in her apartment," Abby replied.

"That's true because of the way her apartment looked," Detective Mallory replied.

"Wait a minute. We did find the note in her apartment because someone threatened her and me if Penny didn't disappear," Abby said.

"You're right," Detective Mallory agreed.

"I also remember something else. When Penny and I started to walk back to her apartment, we heard a crash, so someone had to be inside."

"That makes sense," Detective Mallory agreed.

"We didn't see who the person was because we were too frightened. We just wanted to dash back to my apartment, but after a few minutes, we decided to go back there. However, by the time we arrived, whoever was there had disappeared," Abby said.

"So you don't know if the person was the body in the bathtub or someone else?"

"No," Abby replied.

"Would you mind if we had your phone tapped?" Detective Mallory asked.

"Any particular reason you want to tap Abby's phone?" Bob asked, curiously.

"If we tapped her phone, it's possible we could locate Penny if she called Abby."

"That's a good idea. I'll do anything to help locate Penny," Abby replied.

"I'll set it up soon."

"Okay," Abby replied.

Detective Mallory stood up to leave. "I'll let you know when we can tap your phone."

"That's fine. I just hope we can find Penny soon because I really miss her."

"I'll see you later, too. I have something to do that just came up," Bob said, anxiously.

"Okay. Thanks for your help."

After Detective Mallory left, Abby fixed a hamburger and fries.

As she ate, she thought about her conversation with Detective Mallory and with Bob. *This whole thing doesn't make sense. Where is Penny, and why isn't there any information on her from the time she was two-years-old until now? I'm positive she's the person the couple wanted me to locate, so I have to search her computer to see if I can find any clues that will lead me to Penny. I hope I hear from her soon.* The ringing of the phone interrupted Abby's thoughts. "Penny!"

"No. This is Detective Mallory. I have things set up so we can tap your phone."

"Okay. When do you want to come?"

"We can be there in an hour if that's okay with you?"

"That's fine with me."

Abby hung up and cleaned up the apartment, and after everything looked okay, she picked up her mystery book and read until she heard a knock on the door.

When she opened the door, she saw Detective Mallory and another man standing there holding a briefcase. "Please come in," Abby said.

"Miss Fisher, this is Detective Rowland."

"I've met you before. It was a week ago when you had the fender bender with Penny Marshall," Detective Rowland commented.

"That's right. I remember that day. It was a difficult day, but Penny and I became friends on Friday."

"That's good you became friends."

"We're ready to work on the phone," Detective Mallory said.

"Sure. I have one in the living room and one in my bedroom."

"We'll need to do both phones," Detective Mallory said.

"That's fine with me," Abby replied.

"We also brought an answering machine because we didn't know if you had one."

"As a matter of fact, I don't. Mine quit working."

"Well, you have one now," Detective Mallory smiled.

Within a half hour, they finished with the phones. "We're ready to leave now, Miss Fisher," Detective Mallory said.

"Okay."

"We'll be able to detect who calls you."

"I just hope this works because I miss having Penny around."

"I'm sure we'll find her soon," Detective Rowland replied.

"This will help, Detective Mallory said.

"Okay," Abby replied.

"We'll also have an undercover policeman nearby, day and night." Detective Rowland said.

"I'll feel safer then."

"Don't you feel safe now?" Detective Mallory asked.

"I guess. I'm a little nervous about the possibility of the man coming back."

"Since you didn't see the man, you wouldn't know what he looked like," Detective Mallory said.

"You're right. I didn't think about that," Abby replied.

"I'll keep in touch"

After they left, Abby locked her door and windows and walked into the kitchen to fix her a ham salad sandwich, potato chips, Cole Slaw, and a diet pop. When she had her supper ready, she walked into the living room, placed her food on the coffee table in front of the sofa, and turned on the television. As she ate, she thought about her plans to locate Penny. First, she wanted to see what information she had so far about the person the couple hired her to locate, and then she wanted to search Penny's journals and the computer.

When she finished eating, she cleaned up the kitchen and picked up the mystery book that she and Penny decided to read for their book club. After she read for an hour, she climbed into bed and thought about Penny and what happened during the day.

She thought about Bob and his reactions to the detectives tapping her phone and how anxious he seemed to be about something. She knew that something didn't seem right, but she didn't know what it was. She wondered if Bob could be trusted. She didn't know him very well, but he seemed okay until today.

I hope we can trust Bob, but he seemed too anxious about something. I just hope he's not involved with Penny's disappearance. *I've got to search for her, but where do I start?* She decided to pray and ask God for help.

Within a few minutes, she thought about Penny's computer and decided to search her computer tomorrow because she might find some pertinent information on there that would help her locate Penny.

Chapter Eleven
Searching For Clues

The early morning light that shone through Abby's bedroom window woke her up, so she turned on the light that was on the Oakwood lamp table beside her bed and checked the answering machine to see if any calls came through. Since the light wasn't flashing, Abby realized that she hadn't received any phone calls, so she arose out of her bed, donned her dark green slacks and light green blouse, and then wrapped her dark green bow around her ponytail.

When she was dressed, she folded her cream-colored flannel pajamas with light blue flowers and placed them under her bed pillow, so she would have them handy when she wanted to get ready for bed that night. After she made her bed, she walked into the kitchen to make some scrambled eggs and bacon for breakfast. Then, she set the table and poured orange juice in her glass. Abby pondered over the last two days and what she should do to locate Penny.

Even though we searched Penny's apartment yesterday, I need to return today so I can continue to search for clues because I still feel like we're missing something, but I just don't know what it could be.

After Abby finished eating, she walked down the hall to Penny's apartment and walked inside. She made sure she locked the door behind her because she didn't want anyone to intrude on her while she was working on the computer in Penny's bedroom. She turned on the computer and waited for the area to type in the password. She typed in the password, and the computer suddenly locked, so she shut it down and tried again. Abby breathed a sigh of relief when the password went through and she could access Penny's e-mail and files.

As Abby started checking out Penny's e-mail, she found letters from women who lived in different states. She started reading through the e-mail letters and noticed that all of the women were writers, and that they belonged to the same online writing and publishing group. After that, she noticed the e-mail letters that she sent to Penny, and the ones that Penny sent to her.

Within a few minutes, Abby located Penny's site where she had written several articles, so she read them. As she read the articles, she seemed to notice a pattern. Some of the articles were non-fiction about islands, lakes, trailers, campsites, a cabin in the woods, kidnapping, adoption, and escaping. She also noticed that some short stories, which were mysteries, had the same themes. As Abby continued glancing through the articles and stories, she noticed a description of an island, but before she could find out the location of the island, the computer locked on her, so she shut it down and restarted it.

When she came to the desktop, she saw a notice saying the system locked because of security reasons. "Oh no!"

Abby heard a knock on the door and wondered who could be knocking on Penny's door since she disappeared. She waited and prayed that whoever was there would disappear, but she continued to hear the knock, so she walked over to the door and peeked through the peephole. She saw Bob standing there and wondered why he was knocking on Penny's door. She also didn't know how to react to him since she started having some doubts about his motives.

Something didn't seem right about it, but she still wasn't sure what. It was a feeling she had, but she decided to open the door and let him inside. "Hi Bob. I appreciate your help in finding Penny."

"No problem. I like her a lot, and you, too. I want to help you both."

Just as Abby shut the door, she heard another knock. She looked through the peephole and saw Detective Mallory standing there, so Abby unlocked the door and let him inside. "Hi," Abby said.

"Hi, Abby. Hi, Bob. My guard, Detective Rowland, saw you enter the apartment, so I came here. Is everything okay?" Detective Mallory asked.

"Yes. I wanted to do some investigating on my own, so I decided to return here this morning and check out Penny's computer," Abby replied.

"I understand. Did you find out anything?"

"I found some information in some of her articles and stories, but the computer locked on me, and I received a message stating the system was locked for security reasons."

"What did you find?" Detective Mallory asked.

"I found several stories dealing with an island, a camper, a lake, and escaping."

"Where's the island located?"

"I couldn't find that out because that's when the computer locked on me."

"I see. Maybe we can try later," Detective Mallory said.

"Okay."

"Let's look in the other rooms and see if we can find any clues."

"Okay."

Detective Mallory started in the bathroom since that's where Penny said the body was located, Abby decided to return to the computer to see if she could access the information, and Bob searched in the living room.

Shortly, Detective Mallory entered the bedroom. "Abby, I have something to tell you, but I don't want to alarm you."

"What's wrong?"

"I found a few spots of blood on the carpet in the bathroom."

"What!" Abby exclaimed.

"Come with me."

They entered the bathroom, and when Abby saw the spots, she started to think of Penny and couldn't begin to imagine what had happened here. She began to feel queasy and told Detective Mallory she needed to sit down. He helped her into the living room so she could lean back in her recliner to relax. Bob brought her a glass of cold water and after a few minutes, Abby could talk. "I'm sorry about that."

"That's okay. Could it be Penny's blood?" Abby asked.

"I don't know, but this whole situation is becoming quite complicated," Detective Mallory said.

"I just hope she's not hurt or dead," Abby said.

"We don't know if it's her blood, so let's not jump to conclusions."

"You're right because it could be the intruder's."

"We need to search for more clues," Detective Mallory suggested.

"I just thought of something," Abby said.

"What?"

"Penny has some photo albums, and we might find something in them."

"That's a good idea, " Bob said.

Abby walked over to the bookcase, which was beside Penny's desk and took out the photo albums. She brought them to the kitchen table so they could sit and look through them. When Abby saw pictures of a few young girls around her age and Penny's, she was surprised because she didn't think Penny had many friends except for her e-mail friends, so she continued to flip the pages until she spotted another photo - a cabin in a wooded area.

"Look at this. Do you have any idea where this cabin might be located?" Abby asked.

"Let me see." Detective Mallory studied the picture and said he wasn't sure.

"I wish I could get into her computer because Penny might have this picture on her computer or mentioned it in her stories or articles."

"Hopefully you can access the information soon."

"I hope so," Abby replied.

"Have you thought about data disks?" Detective Mallory asked.

"No, I haven't, but I can check them now to see if she has them labeled."

They went to the desk and opened the storage boxes, and as Abby searched through the disks, she was stumped again because Penny hadn't labeled anything. She'd have to go through every disk in order to find out any information, so she knew it would take her awhile. "I can't believe Penny didn't label her disks because she's organized with other things. She told me how she organized her writing and her journals, so this doesn't make sense unless she hasn't had time to organize her files."

"Maybe she didn't want anyone to know what was on her disks."

"That's possible because she does have them labeled with numbers, so maybe there's a list of her disks on the computer or in her desk drawers?" Abby suggested.

"Check her desk drawers to see if there's a list," Detective Mallory said.

Abby glanced in her desk drawers for a list, but she couldn't find anything, so they decided to look through Penny's address book to see if they could find anything. Abby came across a few entries: Abe and Annie, James and Julie, Ron, Bill, and Evan. "There are several names and phone numbers, but there are no addresses, so I'm going to call the phone numbers and see what I come up with."

After she called the numbers, Abby couldn't believe the results – none of the phone numbers worked.

"All of the clues seem to be leading us to dead ends," Detective Mallory commented.

"I know," Bob replied. "Abby, do you have any idea where Penny might be?"

"Not really."

"Let's take our list of clues and the photo albums and see if we are missing anything," Detective Mallory suggested.

"Okay. Let's take them back to my apartment and look through them," Abby said.

They walked back to Abby's apartment and sat at the kitchen table.

Clues They Found in Penny's Apartment:

(1) Names of People: Abe and Annie, James and Julie, Ron, Bill, and Evan. Phones disconnected.

(2) A cabin in the woods

(3) Trailer

(4) Campsite

(5) Lake

(6) Island

(7) Computer stories

(8) Unlabeled disks

(9) Blood stains

"Let's think about each clue to see if we could eliminate any of them, and then we need to do an extended search on the clues we think will lead us to Penny."

"Sounds like a good plan to me," Abby replied.

"First, we found names of people without last names, and then we found out their phones were disconnected. After that, if we need to continue our search on the important clues and see what else we can find out. We also need to find out how they knew Penny and see who were friends, relatives, or enemies were."

"I agree," Abby replied.

"We also found clues about a trailer, campsite, lake, and island, and those things could be related to Penny's disappearance, or they could be in an area nearby," Detective Mallory added.

"I think those things are related," Abby said. "There must be something else on her computer, or maybe she had some hidden files somewhere on her computer or on the disks. Also, what about the blood stains?"

"What about the stains?" Detective Mallory asked.

"Were the blood stains just in the bathroom or in the other rooms?"

"Now that you mentioned it, I think they were just in the bathroom."

"How can the blood stains just be in the bathroom if Penny was hurt?" Abby asked.

"That's a good question because if she was hurt in the bathroom and carried off, there'd be blood stains in the living room and the hallway," Detective Mallory said.

"Maybe she had a nosebleed," Abby suggested.

"That's possible," Detective Mallory said. "We can probably eliminate that clue."

"It looks like we need to concentrate on the people, computer files, the campsite, trailer, island, cabin, and lake," Bob suggested.

"I agree, so while I question the other tenants, you can search Penny's computer and see what you come up with," Detective Mallory said.

"Wait!" Abby exclaimed.

"What?" Detective Mallory asked.

"Wasn't there a man named Abe and a woman named Annie?"

"You're right," Detective Mallory agreed.

"Could they be the same people who are listed in Penny's address book?"

"That's possible."

"Maybe they were involved in the break-in?" Abby suggested.

"I think I'll keep an eye on them after I talk to Mr. Martin."

"Okay. I'll go back to Penny's apartment and see what else I can find after I fix me some lunch," Abby replied.

After Detective Mallory left, Abby locked the door and walked into the kitchen to heat up a TV dinner, so she could return to Penny's apartment to try and access the computer again. When Abby's dinner was ready, she sat at the kitchen table to eat, and then she cleaned up the kitchen as soon as she finished eating. She picked up her purse and keys and locked the door. Then, she walked down the hall to Penny's apartment and locked the door after she closed it behind her. She turned on the computer again, and when she came to the password, she entered it, but she couldn't access any information again.

Within a few minutes, she heard a knock on the door, and when she opened the door, she saw Detective Mallory standing there.

"Hi, Detective Mallory. I just tried Penny's computer again, but I still couldn't access any information."

"I found out something, so let's go back to your apartment."

"Okay."

Chapter Twelve
More Clues

When Detective Mallory, Bob, and Abby returned to Abby's apartment, they sat down and discussed the clues because they wanted to make sure they didn't miss anything.

"What did you find out?" Abby asked.

"Mr. Martin informed me that Abe Salters is from California."

"What!" Abby exclaimed.

"That's true, so they must be connected to Penny somehow because they're listed in her book."

"You're right, so what do you want to do next?"

"I'd like to know the connection between the Salters and Penny," Detective Mallory commented.

"I would, too," Abby said. "I wondered about them the other day."

"What do you mean?"

"I wondered if they kidnapped Penny when she was two-years-old."

"Penny was kidnapped when she was two?" Bob asked, with a surprised look.

"It's possible," Abby replied. "We don't know for sure, yet."

"My next step is to investigate Abe Salters. Then, I'll let you know what I find out, but before I do that I want to go over the clues we have," Detective Mallory said.

"Okay," Abby said.

"So far we have the these clues: a lake, campsite, trailer, cabin, island, man and woman, computer stories and articles, disks, blood stain, Abe Salters, and Annie Salyers."

"Right," Abby replied. "Do you think any of these clues could lead us to Penny?"

"I'm not sure about the lake, campsite, trailer, cabin, and island, but there seems to be some kind of relationship with those clues. However, we still don't know where they're located, and her stories and articles that are stored on the computer seem to have some clues, but I'm still not positive about Abe Salters and Annie Salyers."

"I'm not either," Abby said. "I know we talked about the Y and the T and how easy it was to change the last name."

"That's true, but I might have a solution. We can have another detective go to their apartment and see what kind of information they tell him."

"That's a good idea. He might find something different. Wait a minute - I have an idea. What do you think about a woman going to the apartment and asking to speak to the woman about some cosmetics that she is selling?" Abby asked.

"I think that might work, and I do have an undercover amateur detective who works with us who can do that, so I'll call the station, and have her come over now and tell her what's happening, so she can go to that apartment."

"Okay."

Detective Mallory picked up the phone to call the station, and within a half hour, someone knocked on the door. "Thanks for coming Megan," Detective Mallory said, as he opened the door and saw a slender young woman, with long brown hair, dressed in a green pants suit.

"By the way, Abby Fisher, this is Megan Parker. She and her twin sister, Christy Parker, work with us as undercover amateur detectives," Detective Mallory said.

"It's nice to meet you," Abby said, "This is Bob, a friend of Penny's and mine."

"It's nice to meet both of you," Megan said.

"I'm happy to help you with this case," Megan told Detective Mallory.

"I need you to go to Apartment 200, and if a man answers the door, ask to speak with the lady of the house, and if he tells you she isn't home, I want you to ask him when she will be home because you have some products you would like to show her."

"Okay," Megan replied.

"I need you to do what you can to get inside the apartment so you can casually glance around the rooms. If you can't get inside, then see what you can find out by glancing through the open door, and I want you to ask the tenant his/her name. Then, I want you to come back here and let me know what you found out," Detective Mallory said.

"Okay. You can count on me," Megan replied.

Megan left the apartment and walked down the hall to Apartment 200. After she knocked on the door, a middle-aged man opened the door. "What do you want?" the man asked.

"Good morning, I'm Miss Jones, and I'd like to speak to the lady of the house because I have some products she'd be interested in seeing."

"She isn't here right now," the man said sharply.

"By the way, what's your name because I need it for my records?"

"Evan. Now, if you don't mind, I need to get back to what I was doing."

"When will your wife be home because I'd like to speak to her?"

"I don't know. I can't keep track of her," he snapped. "Now, I have to get going," he replied, as he shut the door.

Megan walked back to Abby's apartment to talk to them about her findings. Detective Mallory opened the door, and Megan walked inside. They sat on the sofa, and Abby sat across from them in the recliner. "What did you find out?" Detective Mallory asked.

"He told me his name was Evan, but he wouldn't tell me his last name. He just said he was busy and shut the door. However, there was something familiar about him," Megan replied."

"What!" Detective Mallory exclaimed, with a surprised look on his face. "Are you sure about the name?"

"Yes. I had a hidden tape recorder and recorded our conversation." She pulled out the recorder, and they listened to it.

Detective Mallory, Bob, and Abby couldn't believe what they heard. "This is getting more complicated," Detective Mallory commented.

"I know," Abby replied.

"You mentioned there was something familiar about him. What did he look like?" Detective Mallory asked.

Megan gave them the description of the man. The man was about the same description as the other two men except for hair color and the small scar on his face. Evan had the small scar on his face and brown hair. Abe Salters didn't have a scar, and he had lighter hair.

"I think we need to talk to Mr. Martin and find out who's registered in Apartment 200," Detective Mallory suggested.

"That's a good idea," Bob said.

"I think it is, too," Megan agreed.

"That will help you to know if he's alone, living with someone, or is using disguises," Abby said.

"I'll go downstairs and talk to him right now, so I'll be back shortly. Megan, I want you to stay here with Abby and keep your ears open for any footsteps in the hall. If you hear anything, be careful about opening the door. Just open it enough so you can see if someone leaves Apartment 200."

"We'll be all right," Megan replied.

"I hope Mr. Martin can help you," Abby said

"I do, too," Detective Mallory replied, as he walked out into the hall.

"I need to leave now because something has come up," Bob said.

"Okay," Abby said. "Thanks for your help."

Detective Mallory walked downstairs to talk with Mr. Martin. He knocked on the door a couple of times before Mr. Martin answered it. "Hello, Detective Mallory, please come in."

Detective Mallory entered the apartment and told him that he needed to know who the tenant was in Apartment 200. Mr. Martin told him that it was a man named Abe Salters. Detective Mallory was shocked. "Are you sure?" Detective Mallory asked.

"Yes. Would you like to see the list of my tenants?"

"Yes. I would."

Mr. Martin took the list from his file cabinet that was beside his desk and gave it to Detective Mallory.

Detective Mallory looked through the list of names and saw Abe Salters name registered for Apartment 200. "Thanks for your help."

"Is everything okay?"

"I'm not sure."

"What's wrong?" Mr. Martin asked.

"Each time I've gone to Apartment 200, I've come up with different names."

"That's strange," Mr. Martin replied.

"I know. First, there was a woman named Annie Salyers.

Then, a man named Abe Salters answered the door, and a few minutes ago, I had an undercover detective go to the apartment, and she found out a man named Evan was there. Was Abe Salters living by himself?"

"He told me he was alone and didn't want to be interrupted because he was a private person and wanted to be left alone. However, I felt like he wasn't telling me the truth because he said he was from California and wanted to come to Lakeview."

"I see."

"He also told me he was a friend of Susan Salters," Mr. Martin said.

"Have you met Susan Salters?" Detective Mallory asked.

"No."

"What did he look like when you first met him?" Detective Mallory asked.

"He was middle-aged, average height and weight, and he also had a small scar on the side of his face."

"Okay. What about a tenant named Evan?"

Mr. Martin handed Detective Mallory the list of names, and as he looked at it, he said, "Here's someone named Evan who's registered in Apartment 202."

"Yes. He just moved into that apartment this morning."

"What did he look like?" Detective Mallory asked.

"He was about the same height and weight of Abe Salters."

"That's the same description my undercover detective told me about Evan. Have you ever seen a woman in Apartment 200?" Detective Mallory asked.

"No. I haven't."

"Okay. Thanks for your time. I'm going to keep an eye on that apartment and do some investigating about the tenant or tenants who are living there."

"Could the other people be living in a nearby apartment?" Mr. Martin asked.

"That's possible. Let me see your register again."

Detective Mallory looked at the register and noticed again that Evan lived in Apartment 202. "Evan must know Abe Salters since he was found in Apartment 200."

"I'll agree. Unless he was there for another reason," Mr. Martin said.

"That could be, so I'm going back upstairs and see what I can find out."

"By the way, another tenant moved in here yesterday. He's in Apartment 220."

"Thanks. What's his name?" Detective Mallory asked.

"Bill Walters."

"Okay. I'll talk to him and see if he knows anything," Detective Mallory was stunned when he heard the name, so he started thinking about all of the people who suddenly appeared on the second floor of the same apartment building as Penny's.

"Is everything okay? You seem stunned when I mentioned Bill Walters' name."

"Everything is fine. His name came up a few minutes ago, but I'll be in touch with you later."

Detective Mallory walked up the stairs to Abby's apartment, and when he entered the apartment, he told Abby and Megan they weren't going to believe what he found out.

They sat down, and Detective Mallory told them the tenant in Apartment 200 looked like the man Megan described. However, the shock came when he told me the man's name. "He said he was Abe Salters," Detective Mallory said.

"This is getting complicated with all of these people coming into this apartment complex," Abby said.

"I agree. I also noticed that Evan moved into Apartment 202 and Bill Walters moved into Apartment 220," Detective Mallory replied.

"What about the other people: Annie Salyers, and Evan? Those two came to the door besides Abe Salters," Abby asked.

"I know," Detective Mallory replied. "Let's list these names."

Detective Mallory wrote down each person's name so they could see if there was some kind of clue.

(1) Abe Salters

(2) Annie Salyers

(3) Evan

(4) Bill Walters

(5) Ron Mason

"Do you see anything in common about these names?" Detective Mallory asked.

They studied the names, and then Abby said, "Yes. I do.

First, we had already talked about Salters and Salyers. They were alike except for the t and y."

"True," Detective Mallory agreed.

"Now we have Evan and someone named Bill Walters."

"I'm wondering if Evan's last name isn't Walker," Detective Mallory said.

"Who's Evan Walker?" Abby asked.

"He claims to be a private investigator, but he's a kidnapper. He has a partner, but I don't know who it is."

"Maybe we should find out," Megan suggested.

"That's true," Detective Mallory agreed. "Let's get back to the list."

"There isn't anything similar to Ron Mason, but we do know that he's a Detective. However, we still haven't figured out his relationship to Penny," Abby said.

"I know," Detective Mallory agreed.

"Now, if only a man registered in Apartment 200, and Mr. Martin hasn't seen a woman, then it's possible the man is using disguises," Abby suggested.

"If the woman stayed in her apartment, nobody would have seen her," Megan said.

"Abe Salters has to be the man Penny saw in her apartment. Now we have to find the connection between Penny and Abe Salters," Detective Mallory said.

"I want to search Penny's computer again and see if any of these names appear in her articles, stories, or e-mail letters."

"Good idea, Abby. Let's go to her apartment and see what we can find out. I'm also going to call the station and have an officer run a check on these names. That might help us determine if they have a connection to Penny," Detective Mallory said.

"Detective Mallory, is there anything you'd like for me to do?" Megan asked.

"Yes. I need you to keep an eye on Apartment 200. I want to know if anyone enters or leaves it. There's an empty apartment across the hall where you can watch the activity."

"Okay."

Megan left and walked across to the empty apartment while Detective Mallory and Abby walked down the hall to Penny's apartment.

Detective Mallory picked up the phone to call the station so someone could do a search on the names they now had while Abby walked over to the computer and sat down. She turned on the computer and typed in the password. This time she could access the information for Penny's articles, short stories, and e-mail.

She typed in each name in a search box when she came to Penny's articles, but she couldn't find any name in the articles. Then, she searched for the names in her stories, but she still didn't have any success in her search. Finally, she did a search in the e-mail letters she had received, but she couldn't find anything there, either, so she thought about hidden files. She knew how to access hidden files, and when she found some hidden files, she was shocked at what she saw. "Oh no!" Abby exclaimed.

Detective Mallory dashed into the room and asked, "What's wrong?"

"You're not going to believe what I found in Penny's hidden files."

Abby showed Detective Mallory what she saw. He was shocked, too. "This case is getting complicated and intriguing."

"I know. I just hope Penny's all right. We have to find her," Abby said.

"I agree. I want to know what's going on with her," Detective Mallory replied.

"I do, too."

"Let's go back to your apartment and share our findings with Megan," Detective Mallory suggested.

They went to where Megan was located and then walked back to Abby's apartment. They were shocked when they saw Abby's apartment door slightly ajar.

"Oh no! Not my apartment, too!" Abby exclaimed. "What's going on? Who'd want to break into my apartment?"

"We need to locate that man somehow before something else happens," Megan commented.

"I agree," Detective Mallory replied.

"There's something I feel like I should share with you," Abby said.

"What is it?" Detective Mallory asked.

"It's about Bob Wilson. I have a strange feeling about him. I don't know him very well, and he seemed like a nice person, but he seemed anxious when we've talked. He also seemed to have something that came up suddenly at different times. I'm just not sure about him."

"I understand. I have the same feeling about him," Detective Mallory replied.

"By the way," Megan said. "I saw him going into the apartment you wanted me to keep an eye on."

"What!" Detective Mallory and Abby exclaimed.

"That's true."

"I knew something wasn't right with him," Abby replied.

"Let's keep an eye on him, too," Detective Mallory suggested.

Chapter Thirteen
Another Break-in

Detective Mallory and Abby entered her apartment and looked around. "This is getting complicated. Why would someone break into your place? Is there some connection between you and Penny?" Detective Mallory asked.

"We're both freelance writers, and we're both interested in working as amateur detectives."

"What types of material do you write?"

"Mysteries."

"That's right. I remember you telling me about how you're working together as freelance writers and amateur sleuths. There must be something you've written or a case you're working on that connects both of you. Can you think of anything?"

"We've been working on the assignments I had received from our advertisements for our freelance writing service. They were different topics."

"What type of writing assignments did you have?" Megan asked.

"I had a book review and an article to write for someone."

"Who were they for?" Detective Mallory asked.

"One was for Callie Green. The other one was for A... " Abby stopped suddenly.

"What's wrong?"

"The woman's name was Annie Salyers. Wasn't she on our list of names?"

"You're right," Detective Mallory agreed.

"Now what?" Abby asked.

"Let's look around and see if we see anything in common with the break-in at Penny's, but be careful and don't touch anything yet because I'll need to call the crime-scene officers again," Detective Mallory replied.

"Okay."

They started searching the apartment, and Abby noticed her living room and kitchen were in a mess just like Penny's. They entered the bathroom and saw that it was left like Penny's except there wasn't a body, so Abby was glad about that. She also noticed there weren't any blood stains.

"Do you know if you have anything missing?"

"I don't know yet, but let me check the bedrooms."

"I'll go with you just in case," Megan said.

"Okay."

Abby and Megan searched the bedroom. Abby looked around to see if anything was missing. When she looked at her computer, she noticed something missing.

"There's a box of computer disks missing," Abby said.

"Do you know what was in the box?" Detective Mallory asked, when he entered the room.

"Yes, I have each box labeled as well as each disk. I also have them written down and stored on the computer. I'll check it out."

Abby turned on her computer, and when she came to the Desktop, a notice came up that said her system was locked down for security reasons. "Oh no! Not again!"

"What's wrong?" Detective Mallory asked.

"My computer's locked just like Penny's."

"Whoever's breaking in here wants to find something on your computer and wants to keep you from finding out what he wants."

"Maybe he already has it."

"That could be," Detective Mallory agreed.

"It will take a few minutes for me to figure out if I have any missing disks, but I can do it."

"Go ahead and search. While you are doing that, I'll call the crime-scene officers."

Detective Mallory called the crime-scene officers, and within a half hour they arrived and performed their duties in the apartment. After they completed their work, they told Detective Mallory they found the same fingerprints that were in the other apartment. He thanked them for coming.

He entered Abby's room where she had the computer and told her they didn't find anything. He also told her he was going to call for a guard to stay nearby.

"Are you thinking the intruder will return?"

"It's possible, and I want to make sure you don't disappear, too."

"I don't want anything else to happen here either."

Abby started searching through her boxes of disks, and as she opened her desk drawer to take out her journal, she couldn't believe it - her journal was gone. She told Detective Mallory about it, and they wondered who would take her journal and why.

He called the station to have a Christy Parker stay with Abby for the next few days, and he had a policeman stand guard in the hall. After that, he had Megan leave.

"Megan, since Christy's going to stay here with Abby tonight, you can go ahead and leave."

"Okay. If you need me, let me know. By the way, Abby, I'm interested in your mystery reader's book club if you and Penny would like someone else in it. Also, my sister Christy would be interested in it, too."

"Great. That will be fun having you two involved in the club, too."

"Super. I'll talk to you about it later. Bye."

"Thanks for your help," Detective Mallory said.

Within an hour, Christy appeared. "Abby, this is Christy.

She's going to stay with you tonight," Detective Mallory said, when he opened the door to let her inside.

"It's nice to meet you," Abby said. "I talked to Megan about Penny's and my mystery reader's book club. We're getting together to read and discuss mystery books and how to understand them.

We're also hoping to solve mysteries together since we're amateur detectives."

"That sounds great."

"Megan said she thought you would be interested in joining us, too."

"I am," Christy replied.

After the introductions, they heard a knock on the door again. Detective Mallory opened the door and saw a man, whom he didn't recognize, about six feet and average weight dressed in a brown suit.

"May I help you?" Detective Mallory asked.

"I'm Ron Mason. I was hired today for this district."

"I see. Do you have any identification?" Detective Mallory asked.

"Yes," Officer Mason said, as he pulled out his identification. Detective Mallory looked at the identification and thought everything looked okay. "It's nice to meet you. I'm Detective Mallory. This is Christy, and this is Abby. I need you to stand guard in the hallway near their apartment. Please keep an eye out for anything suspicious. By the way, how long have you been a detective?"

"Six months. I also want to be a police artist, and I believe I would be a good artist. My drawings would help you find the suspects."

"Okay. You seem confident in your abilities, and I like that in a person."

"Thanks."

"I can use an artist, so I'd be happy to hire you for that job, too."

"Thanks."

"I'm going to be leaving soon, but please call me immediately if you need help."

"I will."

"Since Christy's here, I'll leave and let you two get acquainted." Detective Mallory said to Abby.

"Okay," Abby said.

"Christy, please let Detective Mason know if you need something."

"I will."

Detective Mallory left, so Christy and Abby could get acquainted while Officer Mason stood guard in the hallway. They talked for a few minutes, and then Abby showed Christy the spare bedroom. Christy unpacked a few things and then got ready for bed. After that, they ate nachos and drank pop while they watched television until. .

Chapter Fourteen
The Photo Album

The phone rang and Abby said, "Hello." She listened and was shocked when she heard Penny's voice. "Penny!" Abby blurted out. Then the phone went dead. "No!" Abby burst out crying. "Why?" Penny!"

"What's wrong?" Christy asked, as she tried to comfort Abby.

"That was Penny!" Abby replied, as she wiped the tears from her eyes.

"What did she say?"

"Only my name, and then the phone went dead. Somebody could have stopped her from calling me."

"Let's not jump to any conclusions, yet because she did try to contact you, so she could try again," Christy said, calmly.

"I hope you're right because I miss her. I wish I knew where she was when she called."

"She'll be all right. I'm sure of it."

An hour later, the phone rang again, and Abby answered it.

"Hello."

"Hi, Abby. How are you?"

"Where are you? What happened? I was getting worried."

"I was on my cell phone, and it went dead, so I had to replace it."

"You had me scared."

"I'm sorry."

"Where are you? Are you all right?"

"Yes, but you aren't going to believe where I am."

"What do you mean?"

"I'm on a deserted island."

"What?" Abby interrupted.

"That's right. I needed to get away after what happened, so I decided to go camping, and then I found this deserted island in one of the campgrounds. You'd like it here because it's so nice and peaceful, and I've been able to write in my journal and write my articles and short stories."

"You're crazy."

"Maybe, but it's not as deserted as I thought it would be."

"What do you mean?" Abby asked.

"I met somebody here today."

"On a deserted island."

"Yes. His name is Bill."

"Oh Penny. You better be careful because you don't know who he is or why he came to a deserted island."

"Yes I do because he told me he had to search for someone."

"Are you sure this guy is okay? I want you to be safe."

"I'm okay. Nothing is going to happen to me, and besides I'm having a good time."

"When are you coming home?"

"Tomorrow. I just needed to stay here for a while."

"What time will you be here tomorrow?" Abby asked.

"In the afternoon sometime."

"Be careful and remember that your apartment was broken into."

"I'll be careful. I'll get more acquainted with him because there isn't too much to do on a deserted island except to talk with someone who might happen to be on the island, too."

"I hope you're okay because I wouldn't want anything to happen to you, and you don't have immediate help in a place like that."

"I'll be all right, so don't worry."

"Okay. At least you have you're cell phone."

"I better go now."

"Okay, but be careful."

"I will. By the way, I have a different hair style and color."

"What! Why?"

"It's okay. I'll see you tomorrow afternoon unless something happens."

"I get it. He's with you now, and you don't want to admit that you did it so people won't recognize you."

"Yes, so I'll see you tomorrow."

After Abby hung up, she told Christy that Penny was on a deserted island and would come back tomorrow. Christy was relieved that Penny was coming home.

"I'm glad you heard from Penny," Christy said.

"I am, too."

Christy and Abby went to bed so they could get some sleep and get up early in the morning. Abby was eager to see Penny again, so she had some trouble getting to sleep.

When Abby arose early in the morning, she donned her blue slacks and white blouse, and then she walked into the kitchen to start breakfast. She was surprised when she saw Christy in the kitchen already making scrambled eggs, bacon, and biscuits. She also noticed the table was set. "Hi Christy. This is a surprise. I didn't expect you to make breakfast."

"I wanted to do something for you since you have allowed me to stay here."

"Thanks."

As they sat down to eat breakfast, they heard a knock on the door. When Abby looked through the peephole, she saw Detective Mallory and Bob. She opened the door and greeted them. "Hi Detective Mallory and Bob. We just sat down for breakfast. Can I get you something?"

Detective Mallory entered the kitchen. "I'd take a cup of coffee, if it wouldn't be too much trouble."

"No trouble at all," Abby replied. "What about you, Bob? Would you like some coffee?"

"That sounds good to me."

Detective Mallory sat at the kitchen table, and Abby fixed the coffee.

"By the way, Penny called me last night. She said she'd be here this afternoon," Abby said.

"That's good. Is she okay?" Bob asked.

"Yes. She said she was on a deserted island," Abby replied

"She also said that someone named Bill was on the island, too."

"Did she tell you his last name?" Bob asked.

"No. She just said Bill. She also told me I wouldn't recognize her because she changed her hair color again."

"Did she say why she did that?" Detective Mallory asked.

"She couldn't say too much because the guy was with her, but she did it so nobody would recognize her."

"That's probably a good idea," Detective Mallory said. "I'm glad she's okay, but there are still several unanswered questions, so when she does return, I'll need to talk with her."

"I'll let you know when she arrives," Abby said.

"Thanks."

"I'm staying with Abby until Penny comes back," Christy told Detective Mallory.

"Good. I'd appreciate it," Detective Mallory said.

After Detective Mallory and Bob left, Abby and Christy cleaned up the kitchen and then sat in the living room to talk before lunch. When it was time for lunch, they entered the kitchen to see what they wanted to eat. They decided on hamburgers and fries, so Abby put the hamburgers on her broiler pan and in the toaster oven. She put the fries in the regular oven, and then they set the table. When the hamburger and fries were done, they sat down and ate as they talked.

"I'll be glad when Penny gets back," Abby told Christy.

"I understand. It will be good to have her safe. I just hope nothing happens to keep her from returning this afternoon."

When lunch was over, they decided to go for a walk, so they could enjoy the cool breeze. After a half hour, they returned to the apartment building.

They took the elevator to the second floor, and as the elevator doors opened, they saw a different police guard in the hall. He escorted the girls to Abby's apartment and told them to lock the door and to stay there.

"What's going on?" Christy asked. "Who are you?"

"I'm Detective Mason. Now, do as I told you," the policeman ordered.

"Why?" Christy asked.

"Because there's some trouble in one of the apartments. Now stay here."

Abby and Christy told him they would, and after they entered Abby's apartment, they closed and locked the door. Christy told Abby she hadn't seen that policeman before, so she called Detective Mallory and mentioned her suspicions about the policeman guarding the door. He told her he'd come over right away.

Detective Mallory arrived within a half hour, but when he arrived, the policeman wasn't around. He wanted the girls to stay inside the apartment while he looked around.

As Detective Mallory started to search the hall, he heard something to the right of him. He listened to see where the sound was coming from, and within a few minutes, he heard a noise coming from the linen closet. He opened the door and saw Detective Rowland tied up and wearing street clothes instead of his uniform.

Detective Mallory knelt down and untied him. "Thanks," Rowland said.

"What happened?"

"Someone came up behind me and knocked me out. When I came to, I found myself in here and tied up. I'm glad you were here."

"Abby and Christy saw someone in a police uniform, and Christy didn't recognize the policeman so she called me," Detective Mallory said.

"I'm glad they did."

They entered Abby's apartment and sat on the sofa. Detective Rowland thanked Abby and Christy for contacting Detective Mallory. Then, he told them what happened.

"Did you see the attacker?" Detective Mallory asked Rowland.

"No, I didn't. I was hit from behind."

"The man was dressed in a policeman's uniform. He said his name was Detective Mason, and he escorted us to Abby's apartment and told us to lock the door. Then, I called you because he didn't look familiar to me," Christy said.

"Wait a minute - You said Detective Mason?" Detective Mallory asked.

"Yes."

"That can't be because he was at the station when you called."

"Then who was the guy who stopped us?" Christy asked.

"I'm not sure. What else did the man say?"

"He told us to wait in the apartment because there was some trouble in another apartment," Christy replied.

"Wait a minute - He knew where I lived," Abby said.

"You're right," Christy agreed.

"Could he be the one who broke into Penny's apartment and mine," Abby asked.

"Rowland, call Detective Mason and have him come over here immediately," Detective Mallory said.

"Mason! Who's he?" Rowland asked.

"He told me he had just been hired as a part-time detective for our district. He also told me that he was interested in becoming a police artist, too, so I hired him for that job, too. He's good because I've seen some of his work. He'll be a great asset to our force," Detective Mallory commented.

"Okay." Rowland called Mason, and after he hung up, he told them that Mason would be over in a half hour.

Everyone sat in the living room to talk until the doorbell rang. Abby opened the door and led Detective Mason into the room.

Detective Mallory introduced Detective Mason to Abby, Christy, and Rowland.

"I remember Christy and Abby from the other day when I was here," Detective Mason said.

"Yes. I remember you being here the other day," Abby replied.

"However, you look familiar to me, but I'm not sure where I've seen you."

"I wouldn't know where it would be, either."

"Mason, have you been at the station all morning?" Detective Mallory asked.

"Yes. Why?"

"Is this the man you saw in the hall a few minutes ago?" Detective Mallory asked.

"No. He's not the one," Christy replied.

Christy and Abby looked at each other, and their expression on their faces revealed what they were thinking. They had seen Detective Mason before the day he came over, but they weren't sure where.

"I'll agree," Abby added.

"What's going on?" Detective Mason asked.

"Someone dressed in a policeman's uniform identified himself as you and escorted Christy and Abby into Abby's apartment and told them to stay there because there was some trouble in one of the apartments."

"I see. I was at the station all morning," Detective Mason said.

"Do you remember what this guy looked like?" Detective Mallory asked.

Christy gave them a description of the man dressed in a policeman's uniform. After that, Rowland and Mason sat at the kitchen table to work on the drawing while Detective Mallory, Christy, and Abby walked into Abby's bedroom.

"Okay girls. What's going on? I saw the expression on your faces when you first saw Detective Mason." Detective Mallory asked.

"We recognized Detective Mason from somewhere else besides the day he came over here, but we aren't sure where," Christy replied.

"Wait a minute - I remember where I saw the picture. It's in Penny's photo album," Abby said. "Penny! She was supposed to be back today, and she's not."

"You're right," Christy replied.

"She'll probably come home soon, so in the meantime, let's look in Penny's photo album and see what we can find out about Detective Mason," Detective Mallory replied.

"Sounds good to me," Abby agreed.

"Do you have it with you, or is it in her apartment?" Detective Mallory asked.

"I have it here."

Abby brought out Penny's photo album and slowly flipped through the pages. Then, she saw the picture that looked like Detective Mason. She showed the picture to Detective Mallory and Christy, and they agreed that it was Detective Mason, but they wondered why Penny had a picture of him.

"This case seems to be getting more complicated," Abby commented.

"I agree," Christy and Detective Mallory said together.

When Detective Rowland and Detective Mason finished the drawing, they gave it to Detective Mallory. He saw the picture and stared at it for a few minutes. He couldn't believe what he saw.

"Thanks for your help. I'll be in touch with you later. You can go ahead and go back to the station or on patrol."

After they left, Christy and Abby wondered about the identity of the man. "You recognized the man didn't you?" Christy asked.

"Yes," Detective Mallory admitted.

"Who is it?" Christy asked.

"Evan Walker. He tells people he meets that he's searching for someone, but when he finds them, he kidnaps them."

"A kidnapper!" Abby exclaimed.

"Yes. I've been searching for him because he kidnapped a girl about twenty years ago. He also has a partner, but I don't know the identity of his partner," Detective Mallory said.

"Wait a minute - Remember the guy named Evan in Apartment 202?" Abby said.

"Yes, I remember. I bet he's Evan Walker," Detective Mallory said. "I'm going to check this guy out."

"Good idea," Christy agreed.

"Wait!" Abby exclaimed.

"What?" Detective Mallory asked.

"Penny told me she met someone named Bill. She also told me he searches for people, could they be partners?"

"It's possible," Christy replied.

"What are we going to do?" Abby asked.

"We have to find out more about Detective Mason and his relationship to Penny," Detective Mallory replied.

"I agree," Christy said.

"What about Penny's computer? I can do a search for his name and see if Penny has mentioned him in her articles," Abby suggested.

"That's a good idea, so let's work on that in the morning," Detective Mallory suggested.

"Sounds good to me," Abby replied.

When Detective Mallory left, Abby and Christy fixed ham salad sandwiches and potato chips for supper. Then, they watched television until it was time to go to bed.

Chapter Fifteen

Where Do We Go From Here?

Christy and Abby woke up early and took their showers. Christy took her shower first, and then she put on her brown slacks, beige shirt, brown vest, white socks, and athletic shoes. After Abby took her shower, she put on her navy blue slacks, light blue shirt, navy blue vest, white socks, and athletic shoes.

They walked into the kitchen and started making omelets, bacon, and biscuits. When they finished cooking, the doorbell rang. Christy answered the door and let Detective Mallory inside.

"Hi. You're just in time for breakfast," Abby hollered, as she finished placing everything on the table.

"That's okay. I don't want to intrude," Detective Mallory said.

"You're not intruding because we have plenty," Abby said.

"Well, okay if you're sure."

Detective Mallory sat down and ate breakfast with Christy and Abby.

"You're sure a good cook. It's been awhile since I've had omelets. The bacon and biscuits are good, too."

"I'm glad you like it," Abby said.

"What are we going to do today?" Christy asked.

"I think we need to go to Penny's apartment and see what other clues we can find that would help us locate her," Detective Mallory replied.

"That sounds good to me," Abby said.

After they ate, Christy and Abby cleaned up the kitchen. Then, Detective Mallory, Christy, and Abby walked out the door and down the hall to Penny's apartment. Abby unlocked the door and entered the living room. While Abby went to the computer to start her search, Christy and Detective Mallory looked for other clues.

Abby started the computer and was happy she could access Penny's website. She started searching the articles for anything that would help find Penny. When Abby noticed that Penny's articles dealt with married life, affairs, children, and other topics, she couldn't understand how Penny could write about something she hadn't experienced. Then, she checked Penny's e-mail and stopped when she noticed a familiar name – Ron Mason.

As Abby opened one of the e-mail letters, she read some of it and became more curious. She was shocked at what she read. She thought she knew Penny, but now she wasn't sure.

Christy and Detective Mallory entered the room. "Miss Fisher, have you found any clues," Detective Mallory asked.

"Yes, but you aren't going to believe what I found. I printed off a letter so you could see it for yourself."

Abby handed the letter to Detective Mallory. "Wow! Penny's married to Ron Mason!"

"What!" Christy exclaimed.

"That's right," Detective Mallory said, as he handed Christy the letter.

"I had no idea she was married or had been," Abby commented.

"This case continues to become more complicated. I've got to find out what's going on," Detective Mallory said, with a determined look.

"Did you find anything in your search?" Abby asked.

"I found some journals, so let's go back to your apartment and read through them as well as look through the photo albums and see what we can find," Detective Mallory suggested."

"Okay," Christy said.

"I'm hoping there will be something in them that will continue to lead us to Penny," Abby said.

"I know you said she'd be back this afternoon, but I'm not counting on it," Detective Mallory said.

"What do you mean?" Abby asked, with a concerned look.

"I'm not positive, but I think she's going to run into some kind of trouble on the deserted island," Detective Mallory said.

"What kind of trouble?" Abby asked.

"I don't know, but it's just a feeling I have. It has something to do with someone she's going to meet or already has met on the island," Detective Mallory replied.

"Oh no! She did tell me that she met someone named Bill," Abby said. "Could he be the one who might harm Penny?"

"I don't know. Do you know his last name?"

"No. She didn't know it."

"We need to find out where the island is located," Detective Mallory said.

"There are three campgrounds in Lakeview. One is ten miles north of here, one is a short distance west of here, and the other one is ten miles east of here," Christy said.

"We can search the islands," Abby suggested.

"Maybe we should look through the journals and photo albums now because they might give us a clue before we start searching the islands. We'll start with the island east of here and see if she's there," Detective Mallory said.

They walked back to Abby's apartment to study the journals. Detective Mallory and Christy started looking through the photo albums while Abby made some ham salad sandwiches, chips, and homemade chocolate shakes for lunch. As they ate lunch, they continued to search through the photo albums and Penny's journals.

Christy spotted a clue in one of Penny's journals. It was a description of a trailer, a boat, and a campsite. She showed Abby what she found, and Abby remembered that she had seen a picture of a trailer, a boat, and a campsite. She picked up a photo album and carefully turned the pages until she saw the pictures.

"Penny has to be here on this island, but where is it?" Abby asked.

"Let's go ahead and go to the island east of here," Detective Mallory suggested. "We have enough daylight left to take a ride out to the campground and search the area."

"Okay," Christy and Abby replied.

They left the albums and journals on the coffee table and put their dishes in the kitchen. They quickly cleaned up the kitchen.

When they were ready, they walked out the door, and Detective Mallory told them he would drive and they could ride with him.

Soon, they were on their way east to the campground. They arrived within thirty minutes. They drove through the main entrance and saw there were two directions to go, so they decided to turn down the road to the right. Detective Mallory drove slowly and the three of them carefully searched the campsite on the right and left. They continued driving through the campgrounds, but they couldn't find any site of Penny or her car. They found the island in the middle of the lake, so they decided to take a boat that was available and ride out to the island.

They climbed into the boat and rode to the island. When they stopped the boat, they climbed out and looked around, but they couldn't see any sign of Penny or anyone else staying on the island.

"Where is she?" Abby asked, with a worried expression on her face.

"I don't know," Detective Mallory replied.

"There's another side of the campground that we haven't searched, yet," Christy commented.

"I'm not sure she'd be there because she mentioned she was on a deserted island," Detective Mallory reminded them.

"You're right. She has to be in the campsite north of here," Abby commented.

"I agree," Christy said.

"Let's look there tomorrow," Detective Mallory said. "I think we should go back to the apartment and search for a few more clues. We should also talk to Detective Mason because I want to know what's going on with him and Penny."

"Good idea," Christy agreed.

They headed back to Abby's apartment, and when they entered the apartment, they sat down and talked for a few minutes.

"Where do we go from here?" Abby asked.

"I think I'm going to go now, but I'll meet you back here in the morning. I'm also going to have Detective Mason meet us here, too so we can confront him together about Penny and his relationship with her," Detective Mallory said.

"Good idea," Abby agreed.

After he left, then Christy and Abby took out a frozen pizza. Christy placed it on the round pizza pan and put it in the oven. Then, they took out their plates, silverware, and glasses. When the pizza was cooked, Abby cut it into slices and put some on their plates while Christy took out the ice tea and poured some into their glasses.

They took their food into the living room, sat on the sofa to eat, and watched television for an hour. After they finished eating and cleaned up the kitchen, they sat and looked through the journals and photo albums. Later on, they got ready for bed.

Chapter Sixteen
Detective Ron Mason

In the morning, Detective Mallory and Ron Mason came to see Abby and Christy. Abby was startled when she opened the door and saw Ron Mason standing beside Detective Mallory. "Come in," Abby said.

They entered the living room and sat on the sofa. Abby fixed coffee and brought out some dainty sugar cookies. Then, she set everything on the rectangle coffee table in front of the sofa.

"What's happening?" Abby asked.

"After last night, I felt we should discuss the clues," Detective Mallory said.

"I think so, too," Christy agreed.

Abby realized they wanted to confront Ron Mason about Penny Marshall.

Detective Mallory looked at Ron Mason and asked him, how he knew Penny Marshall.

Shocked by the question, Ron hesitated before he answered it, and then he said that Penny was not who she claimed to be. Abby and Christy looked at each other and then at Detective Mallory. "What do you mean?" Ron Mason asked. Detective Mallory, Abby, and Christy knew the truth because of the e-mail letter.

"I think you know what we mean," Detective Mallory replied.

After Ron Mason hesitated a few minutes, he said, "Okay. Her name is Susan Mason, and she's my wife."

"Your wife!" Abby exclaimed.

"Yes. We live in California, but something frightened her, and she left without telling me."

"What was it?" Christy asked.

"I don't know because she wouldn't talk about it."

"How did you track her here?" Abby asked.

"I hired a private investigator to find her. We knew she came to Lakeview because we found some travel folders on the floor, and she had the folder, Lakeview, circled in red. We assumed she dropped them accidentally, but the private investigator came to Kansas, and since I knew her e-mail address, I've been able to write to her, but she hadn't responded, so I decided to come after her myself. When we searched her apartment, I saw her picture and knew I had found her."

"You searched her apartment!" Detective Mallory exclaimed.

"Yes, but that was after the intruder entered her apartment and turned everything upside down."

"Do you know who the intruder might be?"

"I'm not sure, but I do have an idea."

"Who?" Detective Mallory asked.

"It's someone Susan knew from her past because I've seen a man of average weight and height watching our house.

I wondered why he kept watching our house. I began to wonder if she was seeing someone else, but then I wasn't sure about that because we've had a good relationship. I know that on his license tag, it says Bob W."

Abby couldn't believe what she was hearing. "Bob W! Are you sure about that?"

"Yes," Ron replied.

"Abby, are thinking thinking what I'm thinking?" Detective Mallory asked.

"Probably. You're thinking it's Bob Wilson," Abby replied.

"Yes. Things are starting to come together, but we still need to know what frightened Penny (Susan), and why Bob has been following her," Detective Mallory said.

"I don't know what happened," Ron said. "One day she just packed her things and left. I wish I knew why, but I've pondered over the events in our lives and what might have happened to frighten her, and I couldn't think of anything."

"Do you know much about her past?" Detective Mallory asked.

"Not a lot. I know she wasn't close to her parents because she never wanted them to come over to our house, and she never wanted to see them. I don't know who they are or what happened between them."

"Did she say why?" Christy asked.

"No. She was reluctant to visit them, so I just let it go because I didn't want to upset her anymore."

"Something must have happened to her in her past that involves one or both of her parents," Abby said.

"That's what I think," Ron replied.

"How was your relationship with Penny?" Christy asked

"Good most of the time. She was a good cook and housekeeper. She worked hard at keeping everything picked up because she wanted everything organized. It's as if she had to be perfect. Oh no! I never thought of it, but it's possible her parents were too critical of her."

"That could be the reason she left because she was too overwhelmed with trying to be perfect," Abby said.

"You're probably right," Ron replied. "However, I never expected her to be perfect because nobody is perfect."

"Something must have triggered an incident in the past, and that's what caused her to leave. She probably tried to block out her past and couldn't handle things when her past hurts started to surface," Detective Mallory said.

"Can you think of something that could have triggered a past hurt?" Abby asked.

"No, I can't," Ron replied, after he thought about it.

"Let's review the clues we have so far," Detective Mallory suggested.

"Good idea," Christy agreed.

They walked into the kitchen and sat at the kitchen table to make a list of the clues they have gathered so far. Detective Mallory took out his pad and pen to make the list.

(1) Campsites – North and East

(2) Island – In lakes at campsites

(3) Trailer

(4) Abe Salters / Annie Salyers –

(5) Evan Walker – Private Investigator/Kidnapper

(6) Bill Walters – Private Investigator/hired by Ron to locate Susan (Penny)

(7) Ron Mason – Married to Susan (Penny)

(8) Journal – Clues about Penny

(9) Photo Album – Pictures of Penny's life

(10) Andy and Patricia

(11) Bob Wilson

They looked over the clues and discussed each one.

"We know that Penny is at a campsite, and we checked out the one east of here. Now, we need go to the one north of here," Detective Mallory said.

"True," Christy agreed. "That would combine the campsite, trailer, and island. Now, we have to see about the other clues."

"We know that Abe Salters and Annie Salyers live down the hall, and I believe they're a couple, but they're using two different last names to throw us off track. I also believe their real names are Abe and Annie Salters," Detective Mallory said.

"They are," Ron replied. "They're from California. I found out they kidnapped a child twenty years ago, but I didn't know who until I did some investigating."

"Okay," Detective Mallory said. "We also know your relationship with Penny."

"True," Ron said. "Also, I hired Bill Walters to find Susan (Penny), but I haven't heard from him for awhile. He did tell me that Susan (Penny) lived here, and that's why I moved here. I wanted to find her and talk with her because I really love her and don't want anything to harm her," Ron said, with tears in his eyes.

"We know you don't," Detective Mallory replied. "We'll find her."

"We also know that Evan Walker is a kidnapper, and I believe that Abe Salters is his partner," Christy said.

"That's a possibility, but I also think there's someone else," Detective Mallory replied.

"What about Andy and Patricia?" Christy asked.

"We'd know more if we knew their last names," Detective Mallory replied.

"If Evan Walker and Abe Salters are kidnappers, I wondered if they kidnapped Susan (Penny)," Ron questioned.

"You mean in the past?" Detective Mallory asked.

"Yes. There was a two-year-old who was kidnapped in California," Ron said.

"I think you're right. I did some investigation on Penny Marshall, and I found out she existed up until she was two-years-old.

After that, she ceased to exist until now," Detective Mallory said.

"Could Andy and Patricia be Penny's real parents?" Abby asked.

"That's possible," Detective Mallory replied.

"I think you're right," Ron said.

"Things are beginning to come together," Detective Mallory commented.

"What name did Penny use when you met her?" Abby asked.

"Now that I think about it she said her name was Susan Salters, but I had a feeling that wasn't her real name," Ron replied.

"If Abe and Annie kidnapped Penny, then they would have changed her name. Now, she's using the name Penny Marshall," Abby said.

"Where do we go from here?" Christy asked.

"Let's find out who Andy and Patricia are and see where they live," Detective Mallory replied. "We can get a good night's sleep and start our search in the morning."

"Sounds good to me," Abby said.

After Ron and Detective Mallory left, Christy and Abby fixed supper and watched television until it was time for them to go to bed.

Chapter Seventeen
Another Robbery

In the morning, Christy and Abby heard a loud noise. "What was that?" Abby asked.

"I don't know," Christy replied. As she glanced out the window, she saw six police cars and an ambulance surrounding the entrances to the apartment complex.

They quickly got dressed and dashed out their door. They looked around and saw a crowd gathered in front of the apartment. Then, they spotted Detective Mallory.

"What's going on?" Christy asked.

"There was another robbery."

"Another one!" Abby exclaimed.

"Yes, and someone was murdered."

"Who?" Abby asked.

"It was a man, and we're checking into his identity."

"Did he live here?" Abby asked.

"That's what we're trying to find out."

At that moment, Ron Mason joined them. "What's happening?"

"There was another break-in. Only this time there was a murder," Detective Mallory replied.

"Who was murdered?" Ron asked.

"We're not sure yet, but they're bringing the body out pretty soon."

Ron, Christy, Abby, and Detective Mallory walked over to the body when the coroner brought it out. Ron looked at the body and exclaimed, "Oh no!"

"What's wrong?" Detective Mallory asked. "Do you know him?"

"Yes," Ron admitted. "Do you know who murdered him?"

"Not yet," Detective Mallory replied.

"From what Penny described, this was the guy in her bathtub," Abby said.

"Are you serious?" Ron asked.

"Yes. Penny would know for sure."

"We have to find her. She's just got to be all right," Ron said, anxiously.

"Ron, slow down," Detective Mallory said. "What's wrong? Who is this guy, and why was he after Penny?"

"He's Penny's father, Abe Salters. He wore different disguises so that people wouldn't recognize him. He kidnapped her when she was two because he and his wife, Annie Salters, couldn't have children."

"Are you serious about this man being Abe Salters?" Detective Mallory asked

"Yes. He's Abe Salters, and Annie is his wife. They found out where Penny lived because they had two spies working for them to keep track of her. They knew she moved to Lakeview, so they hired

Evan Walker and Bob Wilson to watch her. Bob thought it would be a good idea for him to pretend to like her, so he could see how she'd react in their relationship. Penny and I are still married, and he tried to date her and become interested in her to throw her off track and away from me."

"This is beginning to come together now," Abby said. "I thought Bob was a nice person, too. He really fooled Penny and me."

"Abe must have used different disguises, too. He looked different now than when I talked to him after Penny disappeared" Detective Mallory said.

"Her real parents are Andy and Patricia Marshall, and her real name is Penny Marshall."

"Oh no!" Abby blurted out. "It was him."

"What do you mean?" Ron asked.

"He was the one with Penny," Abby replied.

"Who?" Detective Mallory asked.

"Someone named Bill was with Penny, so it must be Bill Walters?"

"If it is Bill Walters, then she's okay because he's the private investigator I hired to find her. Did she say where they were?" Ron asked.

"On a deserted island."

"I think I know where it is," Ron said.

"We think it's the island north of here because we already checked the island east of here," Abby said.

"I think we need to check the island north of here," Detective Mallory suggested.

"I do, too," Ron said. "Also, Bob hasn't seen me, yet, so he doesn't know I'm here and told you about him. What are we going to do about him?" Ron asked.

"I have a suggestion," Christy said. "Ron, you can go into the bedroom and stay there until Bob leaves."

"That's a good idea. I'll do that."

When they heard a knock on the door, Ron entered the bedroom and closed the door while Abby opened the door. "Hi Bob, how are you today?"

"I'm doing okay. Have you heard anything from Penny, yet?"

"We think she's in the campsite north of here," Christy replied.

"Really. Are you going to go there and try to find her?"

"Yes. We're getting ready to leave in a few minutes."

"That sounds good to me. Since it's a large campsite, I can go ahead and begin the search. I'll meet you there," Bob said.

"Okay," Christy replied.

Bob left, and Ron walked into the living room. "He's going to try to locate her before we do. I'm positive she's on the deserted island instead of hiding somewhere on the main campsite," Ron said.

"Let's go," Abby said.

Abby, Christy, Ron, and Detective Mallory left for the island. Detective Mallory took his car, and the others went with Ron in his car. They hoped they would arrive before Bob or Evan did.

Chapter Eighteen

The Deserted Island – Or Is It?

The story switches to Penny and her experiences when she left Abby's apartment on Tuesday morning.

After the intruder broke into Penny's apartment, Penny knew she had to escape. She drove her van to Lake Oakwood, which was in the north section of Lakeview.

Lake Oakwood was an average size campsite where people put up tents, built campfires for cooking and keeping warm, and relaxed in the cool evenings under the moonlight or in their tents.

Most people who camped out wanted a place to escape from the circumstances of their daily lives. Shelter houses were also available for those who wanted to camp out as a group. People could park their cars or campers inside the carports, or in the parking spaces near their tents. Oak trees surrounded some of the parking spaces so people could have their privacy.

Several oak trees almost filled the island that was in the middle of the lake. People assumed that the island was deserted since they didn't see much activity on the island. Most people who took their boats out on the lake went for boat rides or went to the fishing area to fish. They didn't stop to take walks on the island. They also sat in their boats or in the camping area and watched the lake glisten in the sunset.

When Penny arrived, she parked her van in a secluded area that several oak trees surrounded and kept her van well hidden. Penny wanted to stay hidden and safe from whoever was after her. She locked her van, climbed into her trailer, and then made sure she locked the windows and doors. After that, she grabbed some cheese, crackers, and a can of pop, and then she sat on her bed to eat before she went to bed. She shut off her lights, except for a small night light, and climbed into bed. As she ate her snacks, she thought about the past few days.

She pondered over the island and thought it was a perfect place for her to hide from the intruder because she didn't want to confront him. However, she wanted to know why he invaded her privacy. Her life was beginning to work out, and she started to feel safe and secure, but now, she's not sure how she feels.

When Penny met Abby, they started working together as freelance writers, and they both had a mystery book published. They also started writing their next books. Besides writing mysteries, they worked as amateur detectives. Penny enjoyed living in Lakeview and being with Abby. She didn't want to move, but she thought she might have to in order to escape from the intruder.

Penny thought about the intruder. *I thought I knew his identity,* but I'm not sure because it seemed like he had a disguise. I wonder if he's still somewhere in the apartment complex, or if he took off somewhere. At least I'm safe here because he doesn't know about this place, or at least I hope he doesn't know about it.

Penny picked up her journal and wrote down her thoughts because she hoped she might come up with some story ideas.

Crimewriter's Journal

I hope Abby's safe. I didn't want to leave without telling Abby, but I couldn't wait any longer since the intruder was nearby. Now, I have to think about my plans. I don't want to move again because I like living in Lakeview and being with Abby. She's a great friend, and I enjoy working with her on freelance writing. She has a lot of great ideas and has been a big help to me in getting freelance writing jobs. I'm also eager to start our mystery reader's book club, and maybe a couple of other girls would join us.

After she finished writing in her journal, she thought about the intruder and wondered why God allowed this to happen to her because she didn't want to see the intruder again. She thought she was safe when she moved to Lakeview, but now she wasn't sure.

Then she thought about Ron. She loved Ron and wanted to see him again because she didn't want to leave him, but she didn't have a choice. Penny picked up her journal again and turned the page so she could write about Ron.

I wish Ron had stopped asking me about my past. Since I didn't know much about my past, I didn't know what to tell him until I found information on my computer about a kidnapping twenty years ago.

Then I saw the name, Penny Marshall, and I started remembering what happened when I saw my picture and a picture of a familiar cabin in the woods. I wasn't sure of the place at first because I was confused. I wish I knew why they kidnapped me. I only know that Abe Salters had someone kidnap me and took away my childhood from my real parents so that I had to live with Abe and his wife. I had no idea who I was until a few months ago.

Why couldn't my parents have found me? Didn't they look for me? Abe was so mean to me, so I don't know why he wanted to kidnap me? Was it for money? Did he want to seek revenge on my birth parents? I have to find out the answers to my questions. I didn't want to run away from Ron because I loved him, but he kept asking me about my past, and I couldn't tell him anything because I didn't know who I was. I wish I could have made him believe me.

After Penny finished writing in her journal about Ron, she wondered what Bob was doing and what he thought about her disappearance. She hoped he was okay and would find someone he could love.

Penny was still hungry, so she ate a ham sandwich, chips, and drank some pop. Then, she fell asleep because she was tired after what happened to her and her apartment.

In the morning, just before dawn, Penny got up and fixed breakfast. She walked around cautiously because she didn't know what happened to the intruder, and she didn't want to confront him.

Even though she knew what he looked like, she had to be cautious of her surroundings.

Penny stood among the trees and looked out over the lake. She thought it looked peaceful and quiet. She also noticed an island in the middle of the lake and remembered that she wanted to check out the island before daylight. The island was full of trees, so she knew she'd be safe and secluded there. *That's a perfect place for me to stay for a few days, a deserted island, or is it?* Penny said to herself.

Penny gathered up her snacks, clothes, tent, and then she shut off the lights, locked the windows, walked out the door, and locked it. She carried her belongings to her boat, untied it, and then headed for the island. She was glad that she could buy boats here because she didn't have time to purchase a boat before she arrived at the campground. Since it was still dark outside, the moon glistened on the lake, and it was cool outside, so she was glad she had her sweater.

When she arrived, she stopped her boat on the side of the island that was away from the main campground. She climbed out and tied her boat to a post. Then, she picked up her belongings including her tent and walked to a nearby area that was protected by several oak trees. She placed her things on the ground and put up her tent. When she had her tent set up, she took everything inside. She was relieved to be away from the intruder.

Penny took her sleeping bag and laid it on the floor of her tent. Then, she got inside and shut the door of her tent. She was glad that she could close her tent completely in case someone tried to enter. She stayed inside her shelter for a couple of hours and enjoyed her solitude. As she lay there, she felt peaceful and was glad she could she could heard the normal outdoor sounds instead of being in her apartment and afraid of confronting the intruder.

After lying in her sleeping bag for a couple of hours, Penny arose and worked on her writing. She was glad she had batteries for her laptop. She turned on her laptop and started writing stories about her adventures at the campsite so she could remember everything that happened. She described the campsite, where it was located, and about the intruder. Penny still couldn't believe that he was trailing her. She hoped he would disappear since she wasn't around the apartment.

When it was time for lunch, Penny took out a ham salad sandwich, potato chips, and a can of pop. After lunch, she thought about walking around, but she wasn't sure because she was still nervous about seeing anyone, especially the intruder.

Penny decided to come out of her tent and stroll around the island for a few minutes, but she walked carefully through the oak trees in case she noticed someone else on the island. She was relieved when she didn't see anyone else on the island. After awhile, she walked back to her tent and closed it up. She was happy that her tent had a door on it that she could close and lock.

She fixed her supper, which was a can of tuna, cheese sticks, and pop. She knew she wasn't eating the greatest of meals, but she was safe for a few minutes. After she ate, she climbed into her sleeping bag. Penny was tired because of the things that happened in her life over the last couple of days, so she was relieved that she could be away from people and her circumstances.

However, Penny missed Abby and worried about her. She hoped that she was all right. Penny thought about calling her tomorrow just to let her know that she was all right. She had her cell phone and knew she had enough batteries for the time she'd be gone. Within a few minutes, Penny closed her eyes and drifted off to sleep.

In the morning, Penny arose and ate some snacks. Then, she got dressed and decided to walk around for a few minutes. Penny enjoyed the outdoors and the smell of fresh flowers, the sounds of chirping birds, and the other sounds of outdoors. She was glad she was alone. She continued to walk among the trees, and stood stiff as a board when she saw a tent under some trees.

"Oh no," she said to herself. "I'm not alone." She stood there and wondered who was there and why. "I thought this island was deserted."

Penny hid among some trees so nobody would see her. She waited and watched the tent to see if anyone came out. Within a few minutes, she spotted someone coming out of the tent. Since she didn't want to be seen, she walked cautiously back to her tent.

As she sat on her sleeping bag, she thought about what just happened. *Now what? Do I stay or leave? Who is this person? Should I approach him or wait for him to come to me. Maybe if I get a closer view of him I'd know if he was the intruder. I don't know what to do.*

Chapter Nineteen
The Stranger

Penny thought about the stranger and wanted to approach him, but she was afraid. However, she didn't want to live in fear. She wanted her life back the way it was when she first met Abby because she was happy, and she looked forward to working together and continuing their book club, but now things changed when the intruder entered her apartment and disrupted her life.

She wondered if she was right about the identity of the intruder, but she hoped he was someone else who looked like the person she thought. She didn't want anyone to follow her from California.

Penny switched her thoughts to the stranger in the tent. She decided to go out of her tent and hide in the bushes. She wanted to get another look at him before she approached him, so she walked to a secluded area where she could see him, but he couldn't see her.

She stood there and watched the entrance of the tent. When

she saw the stranger coming out of the tent, she didn't recognize him, so she approached him. He was average height and weight and seemed okay.

"Hi. My name is Penny."

"I know. I mean I'm Evan Walker."

"What did you mean when you said, I know?"

"Nothing. I just meant to say my name."

"Okay. I was beginning to think you knew me."

"Nope."

"What are you doing on the island?" Penny asked.

"Looking ..."

"Looking for what," Penny interrupted.

"Looking for a quiet place to escape and to think, but I found the place. What about you?"

"The same thing. I've had so much turmoil in my life that I needed to escape."

"It's interesting how we both ended up on the same island," Evan commented.

"True. I thought I was coming to a deserted island. How about you?"

"No. I mean yes."

"You sure change your mind a lot. Are you all right?" Penny observed.

"Yes. I guess I just answer too quickly without thinking."

"That's okay."

"How long are you planning on staying here?" Evan asked.

"I don't know. How about you?"

"It depends."

"Depends on what?" Penny asked.

"How I feel?"

"I see."

"Would you like to walk around for awhile?" Evan asked

"Sure."

They walked around for a half hour and talked. Within a few minutes, they saw Penny's boat, and Evan asked Penny if the boat was hers. She told him it was. He told her that his was on the other side of the island.

After a few more minutes, they separated and returned to their tents. Penny was glad she was back inside her tent. As she got out some chips and a pop, she thought of the guy she just met. *He said his name was Evan Walker. I wonder who he is. Maybe I should be careful of him, so I don't end up in trouble.*

Then, she stretched out on her sleeping bag to eat and relax. She wanted to get a good night's sleep, but she kept thinking about Evan and knew she had to be careful. She moved so she could escape from her past in California, and now her past caught up with her, or at least it seemed that way.

When Penny woke up the next morning, she ate a cinnamon roll and drank a can of fruit punch. After she ate, she walked outside and looked around. She decided to walk in the direction of Evan's tent. When she arrived at the location, she noticed, the tent was gone. Penny looked all around and didn't see anyone. *Where is he? Why did he leave?* Penny asked herself.

She walked around the island and thought about the stranger and his disappearing act. She wondered if he had to leave in a hurry, or if he was a criminal, but she didn't think he was because he seemed so nice.

However, she felt that there was something familiar about him. She had a feeling she had met him before, but she didn't know where or when. She wasn't sure if she met him in Lakeview or in California.

She also thought he might have looked like someone she knew. Penny hoped that nobody followed her from California. Just to be safe, Penny decided to pack up her camping gear and move to her trailer. She put everything in her boat, and then she went to the area near her trailer.

When she arrived, she stopped her boat and carried everything to her trailer. She unlocked her trailer, took everything inside, and locked the door. Penny was relieved to be inside her trailer because she felt safer. After she ate a snack, she got ready for bed and started writing in her journal.

Chapter Twenty
Another Stranger

The next morning, Penny got up and fixed something to eat. Then, she decided to pack a few things and go back to the island. She locked her trailer and walked to her boat. After that, she headed for the island.

When she arrived, she stopped her boat, picked up the backpacks and cooler, and walked to a nearby area that looked hidden. She put up her tent and brought her things inside. After she shut her door, she tied it because she wanted to feel safe. She still felt insecure in her new home especially since an intruder broke into her home and when she saw the intruder lying in her bathtub.

In the afternoon, Penny decided to take walk around. She enjoyed being outside in the fresh air. Within a few minutes, she saw another tent. She thought Evan was back, but when she saw the stranger exit his tent, she saw a resemblance.

However, it wasn't the same person. At least that's what she thought because he had darker, and it was shorter. Penny decided to meet him, so she came out of her hidden area and walked over to him. "Hi. I'm Penny."

"It's nice to meet you. I'm Bill."

"When did you come to the island?"

"Early this morning. How about you?"

"I just arrived," Penny replied.

"I did, too. I have plenty of supplies, and besides, who needs money here? If I find that I'm running out of supplies, and I need to stay longer, I'll just hop in my boat and return to my camper for more supplies and come back."

"So you don't have any definite plans, yet?" Penny asked.

"Nope. I'm free. I don't plan on returning for a long time because I couldn't stand the hassle I've been getting."

"I know what you mean. Well, I better get back to my tent before it gets too dark, Penny said.

"Okay. Maybe I'll see you in the morning. Sounds good to me."

On the way back to her tent, she thought about the guy and wondered what he did for an occupation. *How could he take off work for so long? Maybe he lost his job. He seems like a nice guy. Maybe we can get acquainted later today.*

When she returned to her tent, she opened the door and fastened it behind her. Then, she plopped onto her bed and thought about Abe and Bill. After a few minutes, she got out some food and started to fix something to eat. Then, she picked up her journal and started writing down the events of her life the last two days. She thought about how she came to this deserted island to escape her struggles, and now she has met two guys.

She was glad that she brought her journal. She liked keeping track of what happened in her life. She also thought she might come up with story ideas.

She always enjoyed writing and wanted to have her material published. I wonder what Bill does? I'll have to ask him when I see him.

The next morning, Penny walked around and listened to the early morning sounds. "Hi, Penny. How are you?"

"Hi, Bill. I'm doing okay. How about you?"

"Fine."

"By the way, what kind of work do you do?"

Bill suddenly became quiet and then said, "I locate people who have disappeared for one reason or another."

Penny thought for a few minutes because something was different about this guy. He didn't seem like the same person as last night. Something inside her warned her about this person, so she wanted to cut the conversation short, but she didn't want to seem too obvious.

"That's a good occupation. I enjoy helping people, too. I'm also a freelance, writer, and I enjoy writing and ministering to others through my writing."

"That's good. I need to head back to my tent, so I'll talk to you later."

Penny went back into her tent and started writing in her journal again. After that, she fixed some lunch. She realized there wasn't that much to do on a deserted island, and she couldn't go shopping because there weren't any stores. However, she was glad that she had her cell phone because she could use that if she needed to.

The next morning, she woke up to the sound of her stomach growling. She realized it was time to get up and fix her breakfast. After that, she stayed inside her tent because she didn't know what to think about this guy. He was different somehow.

Chapter Twenty-One
Somebody Help Me!

"Move out of the boat," Evan ordered.

"What are you going to do to me?"

"Never mind. You'll find out soon enough."

"Why do you want to harm me?"

"Shut up and get moving."

"Where? Over to a tree in the woods. I'm going to tie you up."

Penny did what he told her, but she trembled all over as she walked to the tree where Evan said. As she stood there shaking like a leaf, he took out his rope and started to tie her up to the tree.

"Now, that'll hold you for awhile."

"What are you going to do? You just can't leave me here."

"Yes I can, and I'm going to. You can't get away."

When he left, Penny worried about her life and wondered what he planned to do to her. She wanted to escape, and she wished she had a gun. She struggled to free herself, but she just couldn't move.

What was she going to do? It was getting darker, and soon she wouldn't be able to see. Then, it hit her. She had her knife in her back pocket. She wondered if she could reach it. She knew that Evan had forgotten to search her, so he didn't know about the knife. She tried to reach inside her pocket, but it was hard.

"Somebody help me!" Penny hollered out.

She listened for a few minutes, but nobody came. Stranded, alone in the dark, and tied to a tree, Penny wondered if there was any hope for her. Would someone come to her? She started praying that God would help her and protect her. She hoped that Evan wouldn't return. Her legs began to ache as she stood there. She hoped it didn't rain. She felt so miserable and so frightened that she didn't know what was going to happen to her. Who would come?

Finally, it happened. She became even more frightened. When she heard a boat approaching the island, she thought he was going to leave her there. Then, she thought it might be Abby. She waited quietly for someone to approach. Within minutes, Bob approached her.

"Penny, what happened?"

"This man named Evan grabbed me and tied me to this tree. Can you untie me?"

"Where is he?"

"I don't know what happened. Can't you untie me?"

"Sorry. You have to stay tied for now. Tell me what happened."

"I felt someone knock me on the head, and when I woke up, nobody was around, and I found myself tied to this tree."

"Who tied you to the tree?" Bob asked.

"Someone named Evan."

"He's not here now. Do you know where he went?"

"No," Penny replied. "What's going on? Why can't you untie me? I thought we were friends," Penny cried.

"I'm not who you think I am," Bob replied. "Evan Walker and I are partners. We came after you."

"What!" Penny exclaimed. "How could you do this to me when I thought we were friends?"

"I was putting up a front. I work for Abe Salters. He hired Evan and me to come to Lakeview to locate you."

"Why?"

"He wanted us to take you back to him or for you to pay him $20,000, and he'll leave you alone."

"Why?"

"That's his deal. When you left California, he thought you knew he had kidnapped you when you were two, and since he hadn't asked your real parents for any ransom, he wanted you to come up with the money, and he'll leave you alone forever."

"Where am I going to get that kind of money?"

"Sell your boat to me, and I'll get the cash for it. We'll be even, then," Bob said.

"No! I love my boat. You can't have it!"

"You have a choice. It's your boat, or your life."

"Why are you doing this to me? I thought you cared for me as a friend."

"What's it going to be, your boat or your life? I'm leaving you here for the day, and I'll return tomorrow morning for your decision," Bob replied, as he turned to leave.

"No! You can't leave me here like this! Somebody help me!"

Chapter Twenty - Two
The Rescue

"Are you all right?" Bill Walters asked Penny, as he saw her tied to a tree.

Penny just barely opened her eyes and looked at him. "Where am I? Who are you?"

"I'm Bill Walters. Are you Penny Marshall?"

"Yes," Penny replied, as she passed out.

Bill untied her and carried her back to her tent. He laid her on her sleeping back and wiped her face with a cool rag.

Within a few minutes, she woke up. "Penny, are you all right?"

"I'm hungry and thirsty."

Bill gave her a few sips of water as he propped her up to a sitting position. "You were here earlier, and then you disappeared," Penny said.

"That's right. Someone hit me over the head, and when I woke up, I didn't see anyone around, so I started walking, and that's when I saw you. I untied you, and brought you back to your tent."

"Thank you for your help."

"I wanted you to know that your husband, Ron, hired me to find you."

"I see. Is he upset with me?"

"He doesn't understand why you left."

"I know. I just needed to get away for awhile."

Penny fell asleep after that, so Bill laid her down, and then he walked around outside, but not too far away from her in case Evan, Bob, or Abe returned.

Meanwhile, Detective Mallory, Christy, Abby, and Ron headed for the campsite on the north side of Lakeview to search for Penny. When Detective Mallory, Christy, Abby, and Ron arrived at the campsite, they drove around slowly searching for Penny's van. They finally spotted her van and trailer in a secluded area. Ron pulled his van beside Penny's van and turned off the engine. Detective Mallory pulled his car beside Ron's van.

They carefully climbed out and looked around. They knocked on the door of the trailer, but nobody came. Ron tried the door and couldn't open it.

"Where could she be?" Abby asked.

"The island!" Ron blurted out, as he looked toward the lake and saw the island.

Ron got a boat, and they all went to the island to search for Penny.

When they arrived, they climbed out and looked around. "Let's spread out," Detective Mallory said.

Within a few minutes, Ron blurted out, "I found her tent!" After that, he spotted Bill walking near Penny's tent. "Bill, where's Penny?" Ron asked.

"She's inside the tent asleep. She's exhausted."

After Detective Mallory, Christy, and Abby joined them, Ron introduced them to Bill. He told them that he hired Bill to locate Penny.

"Where's Penny?" Abby asked.

"She's inside the tent asleep. She's okay," Bill told her.

"I'm glad you found her," Ron told Bill.

"When I found her, I untied her, and she talked a little, but she passed out, so I carried her to her tent, sat her up, gave her some water, and then wiped her face with a cool cloth. After that, she fell asleep. Penny had just passed out from exhaustion," Bill said. "I'm exhausted, too because someone knocked me out, and when I came conscious again, I walked around for Penny and that's when I found her tied to the tree. Evan and Bob must have tied her to the tree, and then someone came up behind me and hit me over the head. I was unconscious for several minutes. When I woke up, I searched for Penny, and that's when I found her."

"Are you okay?" Ron asked.

"Yes. I just have a lousy headache and a bump on the top of my head," Bill replied.

"Penny's probably dehydrated, so we should take her to the hospital. I want you to be checked out, too, Bill," Ron said.

"Okay," Bill replied. He knew better than to argue with Ron because he'd lose. "I still don't know what happened to Evan or Bob. I couldn't see them after I found Penny."

"That's okay, Bill. We'll find them," Detective Mallory said, as he took out his cell phone and called the station about Evan and Bob so they could put out a warrant for their arrest. He also put out a warrant for Abe and Annie Salters for kidnapping. Then, he had someone contact Andy and Patricia Marshall to let them know they found Penny.

"Let's get her into her van and get her to the hospital," Ron said.

Ron carried Penny to her boat and they headed for the main shore. Bill and Ron put Penny into her van, and then they climbed inside. Detective Mallory took Christy and Abby in his car.

The emergency room was busy that night. Detective Mallory, Ron, Bill, Christy, and Abby waited in the waiting room. It seemed like hours to them before they knew anything.

After waiting two hours, the doctor appeared and told them that Penny was going to be staying for a few days. "She was still asleep because of exhaustion and dehydration, but they expected her to fully recover," the doctor said.

Ron told the doctor that he wanted to stay with her that night, and then he suggested that the others go home and get a good night's sleep.

After they left, Ron went back to Penny's room. Ron sat right beside her the rest of the night. He stared at her and thought about how she changed her appearance. He liked her hair short and the darker color. He sat there and hoped how much he'd like to talk to her and wished she'd wake up soon.

Chapter Twenty-Three
A Happy Reunion – Or Is It?

In the morning, when Ron felt Penny squeeze his hand, he looked up at Penny, and for the first time since Penny left, their eyes made contact. They both stared at each other in silence. Finally, Penny spoke. "Where am I?"

"In the hospital. We found you on a deserted island. You were tied to a tree."

"I'm so weak and tired. Why?"

"You were dehydrated, and we almost lost you. I have someone here who wants to see you."

Shortly Abby entered the room and walked to the side of Penny's bed. Penny looked at Abby and smiled. "Penny, are you okay?"

"I'm getting better. I'm just tired and glad to be lying down."

The nurse came in and checked Penny's vital signs. "She's going to be okay, and you can stay as long as you want."

"Thank you," Ron said.

Detective Mallory, Abby, Christy, and Megan all came to the hospital to see how Penny was doing.

"Hi. Penny's going to be okay. She woke up a few minutes ago and then fell asleep again," Ron told them.

"Ron, why don't we get something to eat and come back?" Detective Mallory suggested.

"Okay."

Ron, Detective Mallory, Abby, Megan, and Christy went down to the hospital cafeteria to get something to eat and talk.

"How's Penny?" Christy asked.

"She's weak and tired from being dehydrated, but she'll be all right."

"Did she recognize you?" Christy asked.

"I'm not sure. She didn't seem surprised to see me."

"That's because she left you and moved to Lakeview. She probably didn't expect to see you, but I believe she will work out her problems when she gets better," Christy commented.

"You're probably right," Ron said.

After they ate and returned to Penny's room, they found Penny awake. She finally saw Ron and realized who he was. "What are you doing here?" Penny asked.

"We'll talk more about that when you're stronger."

"Why am I here?"

"You were held captive on a deserted island, and we found you and brought you here."

"Abby!" Penny exclaimed, when she saw Abby enter the room.

"Hi, Penny. How are you feeling?"

"I'm doing okay. When can I go home?"

"Soon," Ron said.

"Penny, I'm glad you're okay," Detective Mallory said. "By the way, this is Christy and Megan. They helped Abby and me to locate you."

"Hi, Penny. We're glad you're okay," Christy said.

"I am, too," Megan replied.

"Thanks," Penny smiled.

"Abby, are you here?"

"I'm here," Abby said, as she walked over to Penny and held her hand.

"I'm sorry I left without telling you, but I was afraid for you and for my own life."

"We're okay now."

Penny fell asleep after that, and Ron said. "I think she needs to rest now, but I'm going to stay with her."

"That's a good idea, Ron. In fact, I'm going to post a guard outside her door because we still haven't located Evan and Bob," Detective Mallory said.

"Do you think they might come to the hospital and try something?" Ron asked.

"I don't know, but it's possible. In fact, I may have Christy or Megan stay with you in case you need to leave the room."

"I can stay," Christy said.

"That's fine, Christy," Detective Mallory said. I may have you both take turns. You can stay during the day, and Megan can stay at night if that's okay."

"Sure," Megan and Christy replied.

After that, Detective Mallory, Abby, and Megan left for the day, and Detective Mallory called the station to have a guard stand by Penny's door.

Christy and Ron stayed in the room with Penny. Within a few minutes, a tall slender man entered the room. "Hi, Detective Rowland," Christy said.

"Hi, Christy. Detective Mallory wanted me to stand guard outside Penny's door during the day."

"That's fine," Christy replied.

"Hi Ron. Is Penny doing okay?" Detective Rowland asked.

"Yes. She's sleeping now. I'm so glad Bill found her."

"I'll be just outside the door if you need me."

"Thanks," Ron said.

After he left, Christy and Ron sat quietly so they wouldn't wake up Penny. Christy read her mystery book, and Ron closed his eyes to rest because he was tired from the trip to Lakeview and the stress of losing Penny. He was glad he found her now and hoped that they could resolve their problems.

Chapter Twenty-Four
Mystery Reader's Book Club

The next day, Detective Mallory, Megan, and Abby returned to the hospital to see how Penny was doing. "Hi, Ron. How's Penny?" Detective Mallory asked.

"She's getting stronger.They're going to help her walk today."

"That's good. When will she be able to come home?" Abby asked.

"I don't know yet."

"Will you two get back together?"

"I'm hoping we will, but we need to spend some time alone so we can discuss what happened and see if we can resolve our problems," Ron replied.

"That's a good idea," Abby said.

The nurse entered the room and wanted to get Penny up so she could help her walk. Ron and the others took the elevator downstairs to the cafeteria to get something to eat.

After they picked up their trays and food, they sat at a table to eat and talk. "Have you had any luck finding Annie, Bob, or Evan?" Ron asked.

"Not yet. Annie moved out of their apartment, and so did Evan. Bob isn't listed in the telephone directory, so we don't know his number," Detective Mallory replied.

"Penny won't be safe until they're located, will she?" Ron asked.

"It's difficult to say because we don't know what they're going to do," Detective Mallory replied.

"I planned on taking Penny back to her place, but I think I'm going to search for a large house for us so that they won't know our new location," Ron said.

"That's a good idea," Abby said. "I just happen to know of a large house with a basement that has an entrance to the outside. There's also a smaller house on the property that you could rent out, like to me," Abby smiled.

"I love your idea, Abby," Ron replied, with a smile. That way, when I'm gone to work, Penny will have someone with her."

"Hey Abby, do you think the house would have room for Christy and me?" Megan asked.

"That's a super idea," Ron said. "We could all live together and help Penny out and maybe even continue the mystery reader's book club that I know you and Penny have started."

"Super," Abby said.

"I agree," Christy and Megan replied.

"Sounds like a great plan to me, too," Detective Mallory said, with a smile. "You girls can also work together as amateur detectives and solve mysteries like the ones you read."

"Right," they agreed.

After that, they walked upstairs to Penny's room. They found Penny sitting up in bed.

"Hi, Sweetheart," Ron said, as he walked over to her bed and kissed her. "We have a surprise for you."

"What is it?" Penny asked.

"Abby knows about this large house that has a walk-out basement and a smaller house on the property. We talked about Abby, Christy, and Megan moving into the basement, and you girls could use the smaller house for your office and book club. We would live in the main house," Ron said.

"Wow! All of us living together! Are you sure you want to live with me after what I did, Ron?"

"Yes, Sweetheart. We do need to talk, but I've always loved you and want to spend the rest of my life with you."

"What about our house in California?"

"I'll sell it, so we can live here. Lakeview seems like a nice place, and you seem to like it here. I think the change will do us both some good."

"Thanks. I love you, too, and I never meant to hurt you. When can I leave the hospital so we can move into our new place?"

At that moment, the doctor entered the room. "Penny, you have really improved, and if you feel like it, you can go home. You will need someone to help you for a few days until you fully recover and gain more strength."

"She will," Ron said. Abby, Christy, and Megan are going to move into a large house with Penny and I."

"That sounds like a great plan," the doctor replied.

Everyone left the room so Ron could help Penny get dressed and get ready to leave. When they were ready, they walked out the room and took the elevator to the first floor. They drove back to Penny's apartment to start packing.

While the girls packed, Ron called the Realtor about the house, and agreed to meet him within an hour. They packed up most of their things, and then Ron, Penny, and Abby went to see the house. Christy and Megan met them there.

They climbed out of their cars and stood in the driveway as they glanced around the neighborhood and their house. An elderly woman approached them. "My name is Amanda Jenkins. Are you planning on buying this house?"

"Yes. We need the extra space, and this looks like the place we need," Ron said.

"I hope you'll think about it before you move in there," Amanda said.

"Why? Is there something wrong with the house?" Ron asked.

"I don't know for sure, but I've heard a lot of strange stories about this mansion. I'm just not sure what to believe. I've even seen the FBI enter the house because they were searching for something. It looked a mess before the Realtor came in and hired someone to clean it up."

"What kind of stories?" Ron asked.

"Some people said the house was haunted, and others have said there is some kind of secret inside the house, but nobody knows what it is," Amanda replied.

"How long has this mansion been vacant?" Penny asked.

"Three years. The owners just moved away without saying anything. Nobody knows what happened to them or why they left."

"Okay. Thanks for telling us," Ron said.

"You're welcome. Just beware."

Ron saw the Realtor approaching them. "I'm Ron Mason, and this is my wife, Penny. This is Abby, Christy, and Megan. They will also live here with us."

"I'm Tom Watkins. Shall we go inside and look around?" the Realtor suggested.

"It's nice to meet you," Ron said, as he shook Tom's hand.

They entered the house and looked around. There was a large living room, dining room, kitchen, family room, guest bedroom, and bathroom on the main floor. The master bedroom, which had a bathroom, was upstairs. There were also two other bedrooms upstairs. In the basement, there was a large family room, kitchen area, three bedrooms and two bathrooms as well as laundry facilities. The smaller house had a living room, family room, kitchen, two bedrooms, laundry facilities, and a bathroom. They decided to use that house as their office and for their book club. Abby, Christy, and Megan would share the basement, and Ron and Penny would live in the main area and upstairs.

"What do you think?" Tom asked.

"We like this mansion, but the neighbor mentioned that she heard some strange stories about this mansion," Ron replied.

"Oh. I see. Amanda's a person who tends to exaggerate about things. Nobody ever knows where she comes up with these stories or if they're true."

"She said the previous owners left without saying anything. They just disappeared and nobody knows where they relocated," Ron said.

"That's true. The bank just took over the house. I do know there's some kind of secret in the house, but nobody knows what it is or where it's located," Tom replied.

"Okay," Ron said. "Penny, do you still want the house?"

"Yes," Penny replied. "What about you girls?" Penny asked, as she looked at Abby, Christy, and Megan.

"This sounds great to us. Who knows! This could be our next mystery," Abby replied.

"You're right!" Penny exclaimed. "This would be a great mystery. We could call it *The Secret of Cedar Tree Mansion*."

"This is going to be great living here," Abby, Christy, and Megan agreed.

"I have an idea. We can call our book club *Cedar Tree Mystery Book Club*," Christy suggested.

"That's a great idea," they agreed.

Ron and Penny signed the papers, and the house was theirs including the secret that was inside the Cedar Tree Mansion.

Epilogue

Evan Walker, Bob Wilson, and Annie Salters all three escaped the city. Nobody knows where they disappeared to, so Penny may still be in danger in their next mystery.

Join Penny, Ron, Christy, Megan, and Abby in their next mystery, *The Secret of Cedar* Tree Mansion.

www.ingramcontent.com/pod-product-compliance
Lightning Source LLC
Chambersburg PA
CBHW050524260626
47157CB00004B/1458